Fitting In

Anilú Bernardo

PIÑATA BOOKS
HOUSTON, TEXAS
1996

This volume is made possible through grants from the National Endowment for the Arts (a federal agency), the Andrew W. Mellon Foundation, and the Lila Wallace-Reader's Digest Fund.

Piñata Books are full of surprises!

Piñata Books
A Division of Arte Público Press
University of Houston
Houston, Texas 77204-2090

Cover design by Gladys Ramirez
Illustrations by Daniel Lechón

Bernardo, Anilú
   Fitting in / by Anilú Bernardo.
     p.   cm.
   Summary: A collection of stories about young girls who as Cuban immigrants to the United States grow in confidence and spirit as they confront painful challenges, meeting them head-on.
   ISBN 1-55885-176-3 (cloth : alk. paper). —
   ISBN 1-55885-173-9 (trade paper : alk. paper)
   1. Cubans—United States—Juvenile fiction. 2. Emigration and immigration—Juvenile fiction. 3. Children's stories, American. [1. Cubans—United States—Fiction. 2. Emigration and immigration—Fiction. 3. Short stories.] I. Title.
PZ7.B45513Fi   1996
[Fic]—dc20   96-15676
                                      CIP
                                        AC

To Abuela Lolita, my maternal grandmother, who inspired me to write through memories of her struggles to learn a second language in the latter half of her life.

To Jim, Stephanie and Amanda, whose love and support keep me going.

Contents

Fitting In

Grandma Was Never Young

"Pollito—Chicken; Gallina—Hen;..."

"Grandma! Do you always have to answer the phone in Spanish?" Sari yelled in her home language as she hung up the receiver. "You know that it's always for me, and most of my friends speak only English!"

"But I did answer in English, *mi vida*. I said *'Aloo!'*" the gray-haired woman explained in her native Spanish, the only language she could speak.

"Grandma! The word is 'hello,' not *'aloo.'*" Sari shook her head, annoyed, her brown ponytail swaying with the movement.

"*Mi vida*, if I wanted to answer the phone in Spanish I would say, *'oigo.'* In English, I say, *'aloo.'* Besides, your friends understand and they know it's me."

"You've been in this country long enough. You should learn to speak English!" Sari's dark eye-

brows drew together. She squinted her pretty brown
eyes.

"But I did study English! See, I still remember
what Mrs. Rogers taught us in school:
*"Pollito—Chicken; Gallina—Hen;
Lápiz—Pencil; Pluma—Pen..."*
"I know, I know," Sari interrupted. She had
heard the old school rhyme, repeated by her grandmother in a sing-song voice since she was in dia-
pers. A million times at least! The problem was,
those were the only words Grandma could remember from her school years. Those and some survival
words like water, help, look, boy and, the most irri-
tating to hear, girl, which, when pronounced by
Grandma, sounded as if she were gargling.

"Just let me answer the phone whenever it
rings. It's always for me anyway."

"Not always..." Grandma looked up from the
sudsy kitchen sink and winked a green, twinkling
eye. The lines in her face deepened when she
smiled. "Sometimes it's Mrs. Perry for me."

"Right! And just who do you think has to come
to the phone and translate for you?" Sari questioned
sarcastically. "If it weren't for me, you wouldn't
know if she wanted you to make her another dress
or take you dancing!"

"Yes, Mrs. Perry..." Grandma continued, ignoring her words. "What a nice lady she is. And what a

cute name she has. It sounds like puppy, Perry—
perrito."

"Grandma, in English it doesn't sound anything
like puppy!"

"Oh! Speaking of... She'll be here at four for
her fitting."

"Who'll be here at four?"

"Mrs. Perry, of course. So I'll need you to tell me
what she says."

"But, Grandma, I just told Julie I would go over
to her house. You can't do this to me!"

"*Mi vida*, it's just for a little while. I don't know
what I would do without your help. You do such a
good job. I can just see it years from now: my granddaughter, the most reliable translator for the United
Nations. And I made possible her first translating
experience..." she mused proudly, scrubbing breakfast and lunch plates.

"What about Julie?"

"Call her back and tell her you'll go as soon as
you're finished. *Yoolie* is a good friend. She'll wait
for you."

Sari took in the whole picture. Her Grandma,
arms up to her elbows in detergent, was doing Sari's
chores once again before Mom arrived from work.
Grandma rarely complained about this. Instead, she
took care of it. Even after dinner, with dishes piled
high in the sink, she would do Sari's chores over
Mom's objections. Sari needed the time for school

homework or to watch the latest popular TV program, Grandma would say to Mom, calming her down.

How could Sari leave Grandma to fend for herself with Mrs. Perry? It was bad enough seeing them communicate with hand signals or single words peppered here and there in each language. Without Sari's help, nothing would get done.

❧

"Lápiz—Pencil; Pluma—Pen;..."

Mrs. Perry slipped into the basted dress in Grandma's bedroom while Sari and Grandma waited in the living room.

Grandma specialized in fancy evening dresses. She devoted her talent to elegant garments. She wouldn't labor over pajamas or play clothes; there wasn't much skill needed for that kind of work, and it didn't pay well. Grandma's sewing was delicate and fine, even though she needed eyeglasses now as one of her basic tools.

Her few clients, though loyal, needed party dresses only once in a while. She often didn't hear from them for long periods. But Mrs. Perry was the exception. Her husband's work demanded that they take clients out in the evening. They had a busy social schedule. So she hired Grandma once a month to sew a new dress, and that suited Grandma just fine. She liked to take on one project at a time, regarding her earnings as a little pocket money.

"Tell her blue does wonders for her complexion," Grandma said in Spanish as Mrs. Perry entered the sunny living room.

The royal-blue dress had a low back and straight skirt that reached down to mid-calf. The slit along the side allowed the right leg to peek through as she walked. Mrs. Perry looked glamorous, even with hanging threads and shiny pins on the unfinished dress. Sari's mouth hung open in amazement.

She had always admired Mrs. Perry. With her ash-blond hair and latest trends in make-up, Mrs. Perry often looked ready to pose for a fashion-magazine cover. Sometimes, Sari tried to copy her hairstyle in the privacy of her bedroom, but she never could capture Mrs. Perry's polish and grace.

"Grandma says blue is definitely your color," Sari told Mrs. Perry in English while staring at her movie-star figure.

"Thank you. It is coming out beautiful." Mrs. Perry checked her image in the mirror, pinching the cloth where it was loose and puckered in places.

"Tell her I can take in the darts a little in the bust. That's no problem," said Grandma to Sari in Spanish.

Sari stood quietly for a moment. Why must Grandma discuss the parts of the body? She couldn't bring herself to talk to glamorous Mrs. Perry about her breasts.

"Go on, tell her," Grandma insisted as she pinned away the little puckers in the fabric.

"Grandma says it's no problem to take it in... you know, there." She'd gotten out of that one and felt relieved.

"I like it better than the lilac silk dress I last made for her." Grandma signalled to Sari with her chin.

"Yes, I think I do, too," Mrs. Perry said after Sari's translation. "Tell Grandma that I want her to lower the neckline in the front like she did with the lilac silk dress."

"She wants you to lower the neckline like the purple dress," Sari told Grandma in Spanish.

Grandma nodded, slicing half moons in the air with her finger in front of the lady's chest. "Ask her if she is wearing the correct bra for the dress."

Oh, brother, thought Sari. Now she had to ask beautiful Mrs. Perry an underwear question.

"Go on, ask her," Grandma said to Sari while making uplifting motions with her hands at Mrs. Perry. "Brassiere? Brassiere?" She used one of her few English words.

"Grandma wants to know if you're wearing the right bra." It was hard for Sari to ask Mrs. Perry that. Sari had a training bra, but she'd felt too embarrassed to go with Mom to the department store to buy it. In fact, bras weren't something she and her friend, Julie, felt comfortable talking about, even though they talked about everything else.

"How could I forget? I put it in the trunk of the car this morning just for this fitting. The bra and the heels. Sari, would you be kind enough to get them for me?" She reached for her purse and handed her the keys.

Sari didn't mind this sort of help. It was better than the embarrassing things Grandma put her through. She supposed she should be grateful there were never any pants to try. She would have to ask the ladies about the fit on their behinds or, worse than that, between the legs!

When the fitting was over, Mrs. Perry gave Sari two dollars for her help. Grandma and Sari objected, but she insisted. Accepting the money and thanking her would be the gracious thing to do, Grandma told her. Sari was pleased. Mom thought she was too young to have a job, even to baby-sit, so getting money for her efforts made her feel special.

"Miel—Honey; Oso—Bear;..."

"I was really hoping Carlos would walk by on his way to P. E., but then I heard Mr. Baker's loud voice and I ran into the girls' bathroom," Julie said, exploding with laughter.

Sari and her friends were chattering about school and teachers and boys in Sari's Florida room, the screened-in patio at the back of her house. The subject of boys was important; it kept coming up in spite of Miss Lindsay's difficult math test and Mr. Baker's booming voice as he monitored the hallways. It was Friday afternoon and the girls were lively and carefree.

"How long did you stay in there? Were you late for class?" the girls asked.

"I couldn't possibly have been late, not when I had Mrs. López for the next class!"

Murmurs of understanding went around the room. Mrs. López didn't put up with tardiness.

"I keep hoping if I run into Carlos enough he might ask me to the dance," blue-eyed Julie admitted, hoping for support from her friends.

Julie spoke only English, even after two years of elementary Spanish. She was Sari's current best friend, probably because she lived the closest and they walked to school together each day. Karen and Stephanie also spoke no Spanish.

"Yes, I know what you mean," Karen said. "I saw the whole gang after school, but Joey didn't bring up the subject."

"He won't ask you in front of all his friends! You've got to catch him alone!" laughed Isabel. On the matter of boys, Isabel was the wisest. After all, she and the Martian, who earned his nickname from his spiked crew cut, had met at the mall three times and he often called her on the phone. Everyone thought of them as a twosome.

"We know that, but it's hard to get them alone," piped in Glori, smoothing her raised bangs in the mirror.

Isabel and Glori were bilingual, speaking Spanish and English, and, like Sari, they came from Cuban families. When no one else was around, the three girls spoke in a mixture of the two languages, known as *Spanglish*. But they never spoke *Spanglish* with their English-speaking friends. It was an unspoken agreement for the sake of those who couldn't understand them.

"Do you realize we have to wear dresses to this thing?" Stephanie reminded them unhappily.

"Yep, they want us to dress up. It'll be a battle getting Mom to let me wear what I like. She has no idea what girls like to wear to a party like this one." Julie took a deep breath.

"Knowing my mom, she'll want me to put on a church dress!" Glori also thought she would have a struggle.

"What if *we* ask the boys to go with us?" Karen wondered.

"No way! I'd rather go alone!" Julie and Sari yelled out at the same time. The others shook their heads, horrified.

"I think I'd rather wear the church dress than ask a boy to the dance." Glori broke out in giggles.

"It is our school dance, you know," continued Sari, stealing a glance in the mirror at her slim figure. "We could go alone."

"I've got it!" Stephanie jumped up from the couch excitedly. "We could have a pre-dance dance. We invite all the boys and there, by the power of romantic music," she spun around in the room with a ghostly partner, "they'll have the courage to ask us."

"I think that would work!" Glori joined her in the middle of the room. "But please,...no romantic music. Just loud rock'n'roll." She shook her body with a silent beat, waving her hands up in the air.

All the girls hopped out of their chairs, laughing and shaking to soundless rock'n'roll.

No one heard her come in. She simply appeared there in the Florida room suddenly, a sweet smile on her lips, gray curls framing her wrinkled face.

Grandma was enjoying their antics, though she had no idea what they were saying in English.

"*Aloo*, girls."

Oh no, the gargle sound! Sari panicked.

"Coca-Cola? Cookies?" Grandma asked them.

Sari shrank in her seat. She hugged a sofa pillow tightly to her chest.

"Good afternoon, Mrs. Zaenz," they all greeted her in chorus. No longer dancing, the girls were now quiet and shy.

"Coca-Cola—yes, no?" She pointed to each girl in turn.

"Yes, thank you," each one answered.

Sari moved the pillow up to her face, groaning in agony.

Grandma brought the drinks and a bag of chocolate-chip cookies on a tray. She set it on the coffee table.

"Eat. Drink. Is good," Grandma said in the little English she knew. She smiled tenderly as they picked up the glasses.

The girls were silent, smiling uncomfortably.

"Grandma, thank you. Can you please leave now?" Sari begged, in Spanish.

❧

"Manzana—Apple; Pera—Pear;... "

The phone rang and Sari made a dash for it, turning the corner of the hallway and beating Grandma to the receiver by an arm's length. She gave Grandma a wide-eyed look that said she would handle the call and needed privacy.

"Hello."

It was Jim. Sari's heart stopped. She sank onto the couch slowly with her back to Grandma. Maybe he would ask her to the dance.

"Mi vida, when you finish on the phone, we have to go to the drugstore," Grandma said in Spanish, trying to get Sari's attention.

Sari half-covered the phone with her hand to muffle the noise.

"Did you hear me, *mi vida?*" Grandma insisted, walking around the coffee table to face Sari. "We have to walk to the drugstore in a few minutes."

Sari put a finger to her lips and gave Grandma a pleading look.

"What? You can't hear me?" Grandma asked.

"Could you please hold on for a minute?" Sari said in a honeyed tone to the caller. She put the receiver under a sofa cushion and sat on it. "Grandma, please!... It's an important call! What do you want?" Her tone in Spanish was sour as lemons.

"I need something from the drugstore and I want you to come with me." She smiled sweetly at her granddaughter, unaware of the importance of the phone call.

They left the house shortly after, in the heat of the afternoon. It wasn't a long walk to the drugstore, just four blocks, but the risk of being seen on the sidewalk with Grandma worried her. What if Jim happened to drive by with his mother? No, that wouldn't happen, she told herself. Even so, she looked behind at the traffic for any cars she knew.

Jim hadn't asked her to the dance on the phone. But the fact that he called was a good sign. There was still time.

"Keep up, Grandma, you're walking too slow."

"I'll catch up, *mi vida*. It's just so hot... Walking in this heat takes away all my energy!" Grandma stopped under the broken shade of an avocado tree in a neighbor's yard and patted her forehead with a lace handkerchief.

Oh, brother. Someone surely will spot us here, Sari thought. She walked ahead and took shelter from the sun under a dense mango tree. At least this way they wouldn't be seen together. Sari didn't want her friends to think she had nothing better to do than to stroll with her grandmother.

The store was cool, but Sari soon realized that her mouth was dry, and she looked forward to a refreshing drink. She would help Grandma with her medical questions and ask her to buy her a soda before they left.

The pharmacist looked at Grandma over his reading glasses. He stood on a platform separated from the public by a high counter. He loomed above them so that they had to look up at him to carry on business. By now a small line of customers had gathered behind them.

Grandma held the purse handle with both hands and looked at her granddaughter. "Ask him to recommend something for my constipation."

Sari's mouth fell open in disbelief. "I can't ask him that!" she whispered in Spanish.

"Go on, tell him." Grandma nodded in the direction of the pharmacist.

"I'm not going to talk about that with a stranger and with all these people around!" Sari said firmly in a hushed grumble, her head bowed.

"Why not?" Grandma said in a tone of voice that to Sari echoed loudly throughout the store. "It's a natural body function, *mi vida*."

"How can I help you?" the pharmacist said to Sari, aware of her role as translator.

Sari knew she had to face the matter to stop the agony. "My Grandmother can't go to the bathroom," she whispered in English, still holding her head low.

"What is it? I can't hear you," said the pharmacist in his gleaming white coat.

Sari's cheeks and ears burned intensely. She leaned forward. "She hasn't gone to the bathroom in a while. She's *conspitated*."

"Constipated," corrected the pharmacist, casually. "There are some over-the-counter remedies she could try. Come with me."

"What does he say? What does he say?" Grandma wanted to know.

"He wants us to follow him," said Sari, gritting her teeth.

The pharmacist stopped at a low shelf and handed Grandma a white and red box. "Tell her to take one three times a day until she regains regularity." He looked at Sari over his glasses.

"Take one three times a day until you're regular," she said in Spanish before Grandma could ask her to translate.

"*Tenk you,*" Grandma said with a grateful smile to the pharmacist.

Sari grabbed Grandma's arm and rushed her to the cash register. She wanted to end the misery as soon as possible.

"*Mi vida,* would you like a cold Coca-Cola? Go get yourself one before I pay."

"No, please... Let's just go."

"A candy bar? A magazine?" Grandma insisted, grateful for her help.

"No, no. I'll be outside. Please hurry up!"

"Zapato—Shoe; Gorra—Hat;..."

Sari dashed into the bedroom behind Mom and locked the door before Mom had a chance to set her purse and suit jacket down.

"What's the problem?" Mom was startled.

"She's so annoying, Mom. You wouldn't believe the things she does! You've got to stop her!" Sari begged.

"Who's annoying?"

"Grandma, of course!"

Mom set down her purse and jacket on the dresser and began to remove her earrings.

"Mom, she embarrasses me all the time. She wants me to translate to strangers about problems with her body and, poor Mrs. Perry, I had to ask her about her underwear!"

"*Mi amor*, this is the way you can help Grandma. You know she can't speak English." Mom brushed her brown hair and looked at Sari's reflection in the mirror.

"But, Mom, she comes out when my friends are here and tries to talk to them, when they don't understand! We were having such a good time until she brought drinks and cookies, then everyone was too shy to dance and carry on," Sari pleaded, raising her shoulders and palms.

"You mean Grandma put a stop to the fun because she was a generous hostess?" Mom shook her head and smiled.

"Mom, I had to talk to the pharmacist about *conspitation*! In front of all those people!" So far, Sari hadn't won any points. Surely Mom would come to understand the gravity of this action.

"*Mi amor*, that's a natural—"

"...body function. I know. That's what Grandma said." She shook her head, losing hope, as she sat on Mom's bed. "Mom, you've got to say something to her...please?"

"You know Grandma came to this country too old to learn English well. You're lucky, you can now speak two languages. You have to help her with her clients. Sewing is her means to earn a little money at home."

"Yes, I know. Sewing is her part-time job; embarrassing me is her full-time job." Sari's joke was bitter.

"Have you washed today's dishes?" Mom reminded her of responsibilities.

Sari did some quick thinking, then said. "I was waiting for you to get home so I could keep you company while you cooked."

"You know Grandma is always thinking of ways to help you. She devotes her life to you."

"Devotes her life to me? She tells me so every minute. '*Mi vida*,' 'my life.' That's all she calls me. It's as if I didn't have another name."

"That's a common term for someone you love. It's her sweet nickname for you." Mom continued to make her point. "The little money she makes she usually spends on you. Right now, she's working on a surprise. I shouldn't be saying this to you, but I want you to appreciate her love and her work."

"Oh, no. Not a new dress! Mom, she never asks me what I like, and the styles she chooses are for babies!" Sari yelled.

This had happened before. Sari knew Grandma meant well, but she wasn't up-to-date with the styles for teen-age girls. Grandma's dresses were designed for babies or dorks. Sari couldn't be seen in public wearing one of them. But she couldn't hurt her grandma's feelings, either. So she wore the dresses for family affairs when she was sure her friends would not see her. Other times, Sari wove long excuses as to why the garment must remain in the closet. Grandma didn't seem the wiser, but avoiding hurt feelings was hard work.

"You must be courteous and thank her. She is so eager to see you in your new party dress."

"The dress is for the school dance?" Sari asked with sad surprise. "Oh, Mom. Grandma has never been young!"

❧

"Perro—Dog; Gato—Cat;..."

One day after school, Grandma called Sari into her bedroom, which also served as the sewing room. The old woman's green eyes crinkled with a playful smile as Sari entered.

"I've got something for you."

Sari had been dreading this moment. She would have to put to work her best acting abilities to spare her grandmother from hurt.

From the part of the closet where the fancy garments were stored, Grandma pulled out a hanger draped with a soft plastic cover. Through the plastic, Sari could see that the dress was the same royal blue she had so admired on Mrs. Perry. This was a good sign; perhaps this dress would be as beautiful and stylish as Mrs. Perry's.

Grandma slipped off the plastic cover and held up her royal-blue surprise. It was made of the same fine material Mrs. Perry had chosen, but the similarities ended there. This dress had a high, rounded neckline and puffy short sleeves. It was fitted at the waist, and from there gently gave way to a softly flared skirt. Only a prim and proper girl would love it. It would make Sari look at least three years younger!

"Well, how do you like it?" Grandma asked with a pleased look.

Sari closed her gaping mouth and forced it into a grateful smile. "The fabric is beautiful. Thank you, Grandma," she managed to say.

"I thought you'd like it. I bought extra material when I ordered it for Mrs. Perry. I thought the color would be good on you, too. Here, try it on. I can't wait to see it on you." Grandma unzipped the dress and took it off the hanger.

It was long. It was, oh so long below her knees. The puffy sleeves and high neckline made her feel like a little child. And now Grandma was tying a bow at the waist in the back!

"What do you think? Now, remember I haven't hemmed it yet. So don't mind the length," she said as she pinned the hem up, barely showing her knees.

In answer, Sari nodded into the mirror, fighting tears welling in her big, brown eyes.

"So, who's the lucky young man who's going to take my granddaughter to the dance?"

"We don't have to go with a date. Maybe that's the way it was in your time, but nowadays girls can go to dances alone." The subject of boys was not one she freely talked about with her, but she welcomed the shift in conversation this time. At this point, she was thinking of not going to the dance at all.

"Well, then. If you chose to take a date, with whom would you like to go?" Grandma asked.

With a shy smile, Sari confided in her grandmother. "There is a boy named Jim. He's kind of
cute…" She laughed nervously. "Please, Grandma,
don't tell anyone, not even Mom, or I'll just die!"

"Now, now." Grandma shook her head as she
went on pinning the hem. "This is just between us
girls."

"Anyway, he hasn't asked me. And even if he
does…I can't go!" Sari finished with a sob, just as
tears streamed down her cheeks.

"What's wrong, *mi vida*?" Grandma handed her
a box of tissues.

"Don't call me that anymore! And don't try to
talk to my friends. You know you can't speak English." She shouted and blew her nose into a tissue.

"Well, why can't you go to the dance?" Grandma
asked patiently.

"Oh, Grandma. Don't you see? Sometimes I'm
sure you were never young. I can't go to the dance in
this dress! I hate it!" There. She'd said it. But as
soon as it was out she was sorry for her words.

Grandma's face showed the deep hurt Sari had
caused. Her unsure green eyes looked down the
length of the dress and came to rest on the unfinished hem, now a useless effort.

Sari's cheeks turned hot. She shouldn't have
said such a mean thing. Grandma had sewn the
dress out of love. Being ungrateful and rude was not
the right way to tell Grandma her feelings.

❧

"Sol—Sun; Paloma—Dove;
Hogar—Home; Amor—Love;..."

Grandma stood up silently. At first Sari thought
she would ask her to leave the room. But she moved
a step-stool to the closet and reached up to the highest shelf. There, under shoe boxes storing sewing
supplies, Grandma selected a metal box with roses
painted in relief. She stepped down carefully and
sat on the bed.

"Come, sit down with me." With her hand, she
patted a spot on the bed for the girl.

Sari sat down, feeling too guilty to question
Grandma's wishes. Once the lid was loosened, the
strong smell of dried flowers filled the small room.
Sari looked into the open box on her Grandmother's
lap. In it were a few aged black-and-white photographs, some letters and cards, and a dried-up
corsage, brittle and brown from years of storage.

Sari reached into the tin and gently picked up
the dried flowers, their white bow now dotted with
brown spots. Grandma held her breath as the girl
handled the fragile keepsake.

"Grandpa gave you this corsage, didn't he?"

"No, he didn't. I hadn't met your grandfather
yet. A young man gave it to me when he took me to

my first dance," she said, more comfortable now about the safety of the brittle flowers.

"He must have been very special to you. You've kept his flowers for so long. What was his name?"

Grandma looked puzzled for a moment. "I don't remember his name..."

"So this was a reminder of your first dance, then."

"No." Grandma was thoughtful. "I kept the corsage for Aunt Lucy."

Sari waited quietly for the woman to gather her thoughts. She was hoping Grandma would continue.

"Aunt Lucy lived with us when I was growing up. She was my mother's unmarried sister, and she loved me and doted on me. She went everywhere I went. Back in those days," she looked at Sari with raised, gray eyebrows, "we didn't have the freedom you have. Young ladies always went out with an adult." Grandma took the brown flowers from Sari and brought them close to her nose. She gently smelled the dry fragrance. "But Aunt Lucy's loving concern wasn't always well-accepted."

"Why did you save the corsage, Grandma?" Sari asked softly.

"Aunt Lucy thought this was a memorable gift, my first flowers from a young man, and I should save them forever as a sweet reminder." Grandma gave Sari a tender smile. "But the flowers only served as a reminder of a terrible evening."

Grandma took a deep breath and continued. "You see, when the boy arrived and showed me the corsage, I was happy and proud. He took it from the box and walked to me to help pin it. Aunt Lucy swiftly stopped him and pinned it on my dress herself. She made it clear that a man had no business touching a young lady's chest until they were properly married. In a second, my happiness turned to humiliation. I wanted to lock myself in a room and never see either one of them again."

"Oh, Grandma." Sari was touched. "Did you?"

"No," she smiled sweetly. Sari could see that the pain was erased by the many years since the event. "We, all three of us, went to the dance and had a terrible time. But I never did see the boy again," she laughed.

Carefully, she cradled the fragile corsage back into the box.

"Can I see the pictures?"

"Sure." Grandma handed her the small stack of old family photographs from the box.

Some showed Grandma and Grandpa in their younger years, smiling at each other. There were other faces she didn't know and one of slim, pretty Grandma holding a chubby baby, surely Mom. That was perhaps the most recent photo in the lot.

Sari examined one of a teen-age girl with her hand resting on the back of a wicker chair, in the manner of formal portraits taken in those times.

The girl had a weak smile and her chin was tucked, forcing her to look up at the camera through wispy bangs.

"Is this you, Grandma? Your hair was so long, and it was blond! I never knew that. It's always been gray, since I can remember."

Grandma nodded and smiled.

"And you were so shy..."

"I wasn't shy. Here let me see the picture," she said, looking at it closely to bring back the memories. "No, I wasn't shy, I was unhappy. I didn't want to have my picture taken. You see, I didn't like the dress I was asked to wear. Aunt Lucy had made it for me, and I felt it looked big and ugly on me. I was trying to hide it behind the chair."

Then, Grandma nodded her head slowly as she looked at the royal-blue dress Sari still wore.

"I think I understand what you are feeling." She smiled at Sari. "I wanted to make some changes to that dress, but Aunt Lucy wouldn't hear of it."

It was time to be honest with Grandma, to let her know she was growing up and needed to take part in decisions about herself. Sari was old enough to have a say about her looks. But first, she must make up for the hurt she had caused.

"Grandma, I'm sorry I said such mean and ungrateful things to you," Sari spoke softly. "Mom says that it's hard for you to learn English; you've spoken Spanish all your life. I know I should be more patient and help you when you speak to others."

Grandma nodded and gave her an understanding smile. Then she asked, "If we could change some things about your dress, what would make it prettier for you?"

Sari broke out in a smile. "Do you think you could make some changes to it, Grandma? Oh, I know just what I'd like!"

She ran into her room and brought back a magazine for teens opened to the fashion pages.

"See, Grandma," she said excitedly, "if you could lower the neckline like this and the sleeves could be made more ruffled, oh, and also the hem needs to be much shorter. See how short the party dresses are?"

Grandma examined the magazine picture. She placed a pin where the new neckline would reach and she pinched the puffy sleeves into the style Sari wanted.

"What do you think of this?" Grandma asked Sari.

"It's great. That's just the way I want it," she answered happily.

"You know..." Grandma said with an impish smile. "I think it's time to remove the bow in the back, too."

Sari hugged her grandmother. "Thank you, Grandma." Warm grateful feelings washed over her as Grandma held her in a tight squeeze.

Just then the doorbell rang. Sari ran to the living room and peeked through the peephole. It was Jim.

"Grandma, it's Jim. It's the boy I told you about!" she whispered nervously. "I can't let him see me in the dress! Don't open the door. I'll change clothes and come right back."

"Of course, *mi vida*."

As she ran into her room, Sari could hear Grandma's heavily accented English. "Come in, Yeem. Coca-Cola? Yes?"

"Caballo—Horse; Vaca—Cow;
This rhyme has ended, Ahora—Now."

Hurricane Friends

Clari swung her heavy book bag over the chain-link fence. It was filled with books she had borrowed from the public library. It landed on the grass with a thud. She looked around to see if Mrs. Murphy had heard the noise. No one was in sight.

The fence was low but hard to climb. The small openings in the wire dug into the tender skin of her foot, in spite of her sneaker's rubber sole. The wire gave way. It bent under her weight and made it difficult for Clari to lift her leg over the top. She held on tightly, swinging her legs over one at a time, and sat on the horizontal metal bar. Freed of Clari's weight, the wire mesh sprung back with the noisy clatter of vibrating metal.

She looked up in panic. In the back window of the house, Mrs. Murphy's face appeared. Her grouchy look told Clari she meant business.

Clari jumped down from the fence into Mrs. Murphy's yard. With a bounce to regain her balance, Clari scooped up her bag and sprinted across the grass. She ran as fast as her thirteen-year-old legs would carry her to her house next door.

Gasping for breath, she banged on her own front door. "Papi! Papi! Quick, let me in!" Clari yelled in Spanish, the language she spoke at home.

"Open the door, Papi!" she begged her father breathlessly. If Mrs. Murphy found her helplessly alone on the front porch, she was doomed. Before long, Papi unlocked the door. She shoved it open and ran in, slamming it shut behind her.

"What's wrong?" Papi asked in Spanish, watching Clari who breathed hard and shook. Her shiny brown hair clung to her wet neck.

Clari grabbed his hand and led him into the house, away from the door. She couldn't tell him her real concern. He had warned her not to climb their neighbor's fence. So, she distracted Papi with the news she had heard at the public library. "There's a hurricane on the way!"

"Calm down," Papi said, putting an arm around Clari. "It will be a few days before we know if it's going to pass over Miami. We can't be too worried yet."

"Papi, I know it's coming! It's on the way!" Clari insisted.

"I'll turn on the television and see what they have to say," her father said softly.

As Papi bent down to press the TV button, the doorbell rang. Clari jumped back. She was sure it was Mrs. Murphy.

"Go answer the door, *mi hija*," Papi asked, using his favorite name for Clari, my daughter.

"No! You'd better do it. I've got to clean my room," she said and quickly disappeared into her room. Clari peeked around her bedroom door.

Papi opened the door.

"Mr. Martínez. Your daughter is at it again!" Mrs. Murphy's voice cracked with age as she spoke the words in English. Her crooked finger was pointed straight at him, like a threatening pistol. "She's hopping over my fence and damaging it. I'm not putting up with this behavior anymore!"

Mrs. Murphy stepped slowly forward as Papi backed into the house, motioning an invitation for the old woman to come in.

This is what Clari had feared. Mrs. Murphy would tell on her and punishment would be sure to follow.

"Clarita! Come out here and explain to me what Mrs. Murphy is saying." Papi's Spanish words had an angry tone to them.

Clari came out from behind her door, leaving the safety of her bedroom, and stood by Papi. "She says I climbed over her fence and I'm breaking it." Clari looked down at her toes, protected by the canvas sneakers. She wished she could shrink and, like her toes, hide inside one of her shoes.

"Clarita, look at me." Papi waited for Clari's brown eyes to meet his. "Mami and I have told you not to do this."

She blurted the explanatory words quickly in Spanish. "Yes, Papi. I know. But it's faster to..."

Papi interrupted her excuses. "Tell Mrs. Murphy you are sorry and you will not do this again."

"But, Papi." Clari looked at him sadly.

"Tell Mrs. Murphy what I told you." Papi wouldn't back down.

Clari translated Papi's words. "I'm sorry. I won't do it again." She looked at the older woman shyly and saw that her silver-knitted brows did not relax. Mrs. Murphy's lips still held a downturned curve.

"I go look at the fence later," Papi said in his halting English. "I fix. I fix," he assured his neighbor.

Mrs. Murphy nodded her head and without a smile turned and left.

Papi closed the door behind her. Clari feared the part that was yet to come. His face was not happy.

"So this is the hurricane that was heading this way," Papi said, shaking his head.

"No, Papi. There's a real storm coming!"

Papi ignored her words. "Clarita, not only are you bending the fence, but what you are doing is dangerous. You could get caught in the wires and break a leg. Or you could fall on your face and need stitches. Don't do it again!"

"But, Papi," she pleaded. "It's a short cut from everywhere: the library, school, the park. If I don't jump over the fence, then I have to go three blocks out of my way to get home."

"Taking the expected route home is not going out of your way. You must not cross other people's yards."

"But, Papi, Mrs. Murphy's not being fair. Our back yard doesn't back up to the park like hers does. If I don't jump over her fence, it takes me forever to get home!"

"Clarita, not another word about it! Go to your room now. You cannot see your friends this weekend. Maybe you'll think about what you've done and stop disobeying our rules."

Clari walked back to her room, disappointed. It was only Friday and she was grounded for the weekend. Papi couldn't see how unfair it all was. The long way added at least five minutes to her walk. And it was hot, especially carrying those heavy library books in the August sun.

Besides, the fence wasn't damaged. It was just sagging a bit. She wasn't heavy enough to break it. Mrs. Murphy was a grouch who complained about everything.

Yet maybe it wasn't such a great loss. If the hurricane came over Miami, she would have to spend the time in her room anyway. She wouldn't be able to meet with her friends during the storm, even if Papi had not punished her.

❧

Mami arrived home from work as the evening news began. "Did they say anything more about the storm?" she asked Papi, setting down her purse.

"Not yet. The weather report is coming soon," he said, not taking his eyes off the screen.

Mami walked behind his chair and bent down to hug him. Her long brown hair mingled with his dark wavy hair. "It's a good thing avocado season is over. I'm glad we picked all the fruit and shared it with our friends. All we need is a heavy green football crashing through our window in the wind."

Clari smiled, standing at her bedroom door. She had been listening and watching TV out of Papi's view. She wanted to know more about the hurricane. But she kept quiet so Papi wouldn't send her back into the room.

"Uhm, it smells good!" Mami said. "You're cooking black beans for dinner?"

"Yes, they're ready now. I have to be at work for the seven o'clock shift. I've got a spicy *picadillo* simmering on the stove, too."

Papi worked at the airport. He carried luggage for passengers, receiving tips for his help. This was a good way to practice his English, as he had to communicate with travelers from all over the country. He worked at night because he got paid more. Often, he would cook dinner so Mami would not have to rush.

The delicious aroma of the Cuban bean soup had been teasing Clari for the past hour. Now, she couldn't wait to eat.

"Where's Clari?" Mami asked, walking to the kitchen. She missed Clari's noisy laughter.

"I'm in here, Mami," Clari said from the bedroom door.

"Well, come on out. Give me a kiss and start setting the table."

"Papi won't let me," Clari said, pouting.

Papi straightened up in his chair. "Who says I won't let you help your mother? You can come out of the room to help with chores. You know that."

"Oh, oh. What happened now?" Mami asked, getting busy in the kitchen.

Clari ran in and hugged her. "Mami, Mrs. Murphy won't let me take the short cut. She came to complain about me to Papi."

"Again?" Mami raised a dark eyebrow.

Clari took napkins and silverware to the table. "Uhm, Papi makes a delicious black bean soup."

"Don't change the subject, young lady. You know we don't allow you to climb over the fence. Besides, at thirteen, you're too old for that."

"I really work up a sweat going the long way. But…if you'd rather do more laundry."

"Don't worry about the laundry. I'll handle it. Or better yet, you can wash your own clothes."

"Here's the weather report!" Papi called from the living room.

Clari and Mami rushed to his side. All listened quietly to the weatherman. The storm had increased in strength and was now called Hurricane Andrew. It was east of the Bahama islands and was headed west, toward Florida.

"That means we have to start preparing for the storm!" Mami said nervously.

"Yes, I'm sure we'll be asked to help secure windows at the airport tonight." The look on Papi's face was somber. "We have two days to get things in order. If it comes our way, it will be here Monday morning."

"I'd better check our supply of candles and food that won't spoil," Mami said, turning back into the kitchen.

"Why do we need those things?" Clari asked.

"We'll probably lose electricity and the food in the refrigerator will spoil. We also won't have any way to cook it," Mami explained.

"And we'll use the candles to see at night," Clari suggested, understanding the need for the supplies.

"*Sí, mi hija*," said Papi, who had now joined them in the kitchen. "But we'll need the candles in the daytime as well. After I put sheets of plywood over the windows to protect us, the house will be very dark inside."

Clari shuddered to think of the darkened rooms they'd be in while the storm threatened them outside. With the windows covered, they would not be able to see what was going on.

"I'll go to the hardware store in the morning," Papi said. "You'd better buy the things we need from the grocery store."

Mami nodded. "Clari and I will go tonight."

❧

When Papi left for work, Clari helped Mami clean the dishes in the sink. Her parents worked different hours, and she enjoyed having time alone with each of them. She had Papi to herself all afternoon, and Mami to share her evenings.

Mami searched through the cupboards with a pencil and paper in her hand. She wrote down the items they needed and mumbled the words to herself.

"Tuna, six cans. Evaporated milk, ten cans. Cuban crackers, two bags. Drinking water, six gallons..."

Clari gathered the bag of garbage and headed out the back door.

"We are going to the grocery store as soon as you finish," Mami said through the open door.

Clari looked around the dark back yard. "Here, kitty, kitty," she called softly. She lifted the lid to the plastic garbage can and dropped the bag in it. Clari banged on the side of the container with the lid three times. "Here, kitty, kitty," she called again.

With the rattling of dry leaves under her feet, a black cat came running out of the bushes. Her shiny coat had irregular white spots which, against the dark fur, resembled a starry sky.

"Midnight!" Clari said happily, getting down on her knees. She stroked the silky fur from head to tail. "I brought you dinner. Papi made a delicious *picadillo*."

Clari set down the bowl of spicy ground beef left over from dinner. The cat licked the meat tentatively at first, then put her face in the bowl and ate. Clari watched peacefully.

She fed Midnight, Mrs. Murphy's cat, every evening when she was able. Mrs. Murphy wouldn't approve if she knew. She let Midnight out every night for a few hours, and Midnight came to visit Clari. Mrs. Murphy insisted on a special diet for

Midnight. But Clari was sure Midnight preferred the special treats she gave her to the dry, bagged food Mrs. Murphy bought.

"Clari, we have to go," Mami called from the kitchen door.

Clari stroked Midnight one last time. She picked up the empty bowl and ran back.

"What kept you so long?" Mami asked as she entered the kitchen.

Clari hid the bowl behind her. "Oh, nothing," she answered.

But Mami could tell something was going on. "You've been feeding Mrs. Murphy's cat again, haven't you?" Mami tilted her head to look at Clari. "You know she doesn't like you to do that."

Clari lowered her eyes and shrugged. "I know. Papi doesn't want the cat to come by our house either because she frightens Kiki," Clari said, referring to the family's parakeet. "But you can't pat and hug a bird in a cage. Midnight is such a cuddly pet. You can tell she enjoys it."

The grocery store was packed with shoppers, eagerly preparing for the hurricane. Grocery carts were loaded with canned food, batteries, and plastic bottles of juice and drinking water. No one was buying fresh meats or frozen foods. The people seemed busy and nervous.

Clari helped Mami push the cart as they moved from aisle to aisle. Mami selected the items on her

list, though some were already sold out. She asked
Clari to get paper cups and plates.

"The water coming through the pipes after the
storm may be muddy. We may not be able to wash
dishes," Mami explained, then sent her on another
errand. "Find a bag of birdseed for Kiki."

It seemed, to Clari, they'd have to plan for
everything.

When she reached the pet-food section, Clari
remembered Midnight. She would not be able to
feed her for a few days. What if Mrs. Murphy ran
out of food for her?

Clari ran back to the cart with two bags of pet
food, birdseed for Kiki and the dry food for Midnight. She put Midnight's food at the bottom of the
cart and covered it with Kiki's birdseed.

Mami looked at her. "No, no. Tonight, we can't
be buying things we don't need. We'll buy only
what's important."

"But this is important," Clari said, her hands
clasped together in praying fashion. "It's food for
Midnight."

Mami ran her fingers through Clari's long
brown hair. She looked at her daughter lovingly.
"Very well. Since it's an emergency, we can get food
for Midnight."

Saturday morning, Clari sat in her room.

There was little else to do. School was set to begin next week, so she had no homework. She had leafed through the library books she had brought home the day before and had styled her hair every which way.

Now, she listened to rock 'n' roll tapes on her portable tape player. Her favorite radio station had stopped playing music and was giving information about the hurricane from now on. It seemed the storm was headed for South Florida. But Clari was tired of hearing about it. She turned the volume up. She practiced dance moves to the rhythm of the songs.

Papi wouldn't let her out of the room to see her friends. *"Don't climb over the fence!"* echoed in her mind. But, she was learning another lesson, too, *"Stay clear of Mrs. Murphy!"* The old lady was trouble.

Papi brought a ladder to the side of the house, by Clari's window.

"Hello, Papi!" she yelled to him over the music, through the open glass panels.

"How are you, *mi hija?*" Papi asked in response.

"I'm fine," Clari answered, waving to him with the beat of the song. "What are you doing with the ladder?"

"I'm going up on the roof," Papi said, taking the first steps up. "I'm taking down the TV antenna. We can't have it up during the storm."

"Be careful, Papi," Clari called after him as he rose up to the cement tile roof.

She could hear the metallic sound of a tool hitting the wrench Papi was using. She waited by the window. In a few minutes, the antenna came loose and collapsed against the roof. Clari could see Papi's hands as he reached for it to keep it from falling to the ground.

Papi started back down the ladder with the pointy contraption held in one hand. Just then, the tall pole that held the antenna up swung back, away from the house, and the whole thing jerked loose from Papi's hands. Papi grabbed the ladder tightly, and for a moment it appeared he would lose his balance and fall.

"Hold on, Papi!" Clari screamed.

The ladder bounced against the side of the house, with Papi hopping on it like a monkey on a tree branch. The antenna crashed into a tree and finally onto the ground. It took with it a branch and many of Mrs. Murphy's unripened grapefruit. The ladder came to rest safely against the wall of the house with Papi still holding tight. Everything was quiet now, only the loud rock 'n' roll broke the stillness.

Clari ran out to the side of the house. "Papi, are you all right?" She could see he was. He was back on the ground, straightening up the bent antenna.

On the other side of the fence stood Mrs. Murphy. She examined her damaged tree and the fruit on the ground. Her gray brows were drawn tightly together. She looked very unhappy.

"Mr. Martínez, really!" she said in English.

Papi's face reddened. "I'm sorry, Mrs. Murphy. It was accident." Papi stretched an open hand out in front.

"I can't hear you, Mr. Martínez. Your daughter plays the music much too loud."

Scowling, Papi turned to Clari. "I can't hear Mrs. Murphy, Clarita. Your radio is too loud," he said in Spanish.

"It's not the radio. It's a tape," Clari corrected him. But the moment she let the words out of her mouth she knew she was in trouble.

"I don't care if it's a live band!" Papi shouted angrily. His eyes squinted as he looked at her. "I want silence!"

She had tested Papi's patience and had stretched his limit. Clari ran back in her room and turned off the noise. All was silent again. She returned to his side in no time. She didn't want to miss the action.

"You see the fence? I fix," Papi said to his neighbor, and pointed to the back, where Clari had done the damage. He was trying to draw attention away from the mess he had made.

"Yes. It looks fine," Mrs. Murphy said without looking in the direction he pointed. "But now, you've broken a tree branch and you've knocked down many grapefruit. The tree is ruined!" she said angrily.

In Spanish, Papi asked Clari, "What did she say?"

"You hurt the tree. You knocked down her fruit," Clari translated. "She's very mad at you, Papi," Clari added.

"I can see that. I don't have to speak English to see," Papi said, annoyed at Clari.

Papi couldn't tell Mrs. Murphy that the hurricane was sure to remove whatever fruit was left on the tree. "I'm sorry," was all he could say.

"Mr. Martínez, you're going to have to learn English. You live in the United States now!" Mrs. Murphy pointed a knobby finger at him.

Clari gasped at her meanness. Papi was trying hard to learn a second language at his age. Ever since he left Cuba, his place of birth, he had been trying to learn. He and Mami had even attended lessons at the high school at night, before he took the job at the airport.

"I learn, I learn," Clari's father smiled. Clari couldn't believe he wasn't angry at Mrs. Murphy for speaking to him that way.

"Mrs. Murphy, a hurricane is coming. Do you know?" Papi asked in his broken English.

It was hard to imagine a big storm was coming their way. Clari looked up. The sky was clear blue. The sun was shining brightly.

The old lady shrugged her shoulders. She didn't seem to care. "Yes, I know. My husband and I went through a few together, before he died."

"You need my help? I take down your antenna. No?"

Mrs. Murphy's eyes opened wide. She crossed her arms back and forth, scissor-style, in front of her. "No, thank you," she said.

"I take your lawn chairs into the garage. Yes?"

Mrs. Murphy shook her head. Her gray curls bounced with the movement. "No, thank you. I can do it myself."

They watched Mrs. Murphy walk to her patio and begin folding and taking in her furniture.

"That poor old lady is carrying the chairs by herself. You should offer your help," Mami said in Spanish when she joined Clari and Papi.

"She wouldn't let me help," said Papi.

"She's such a grouch," Clari whispered in Spanish. "She told you to learn English and she hardly thanked you for fixing the fence."

"*Mi hija*, I fixed the fence because you bent it. It's the least I could do. She can't be too grateful for that."

"My music bothered her. Everything bothers her," Clari shook her head, annoyed.

"You *do* play your music too loud," Mami said, smiling. "It bothers even me."

Clari laughed. But she was puzzled. She turned to Papi, who was folding the ladder. "Why doesn't Mrs. Murphy let you help her?"

Papi was thoughtful for a moment. "I think she is a very independent person. She's used to doing everything by herself."

"She's grouchy, Papi!" Clari would not be convinced.

"I think Mrs. Murphy is a little lonely," Mami corrected.

Papi carried the ladder under his arm. "Come to the garage with me and get a bucket for the grapefruit on the ground. They're not any good now. All we can do for our neighbor is clean up the mess."

"When you finish, you can help me bring in my potted plants," Mami said to Clari as she walked away.

"Even the pots have to be taken inside?" Clari asked in disbelief.

"Anything that's loose can be picked up by the hurricane winds. Then it becomes a flying weapon," Mami said, nodding.

Sunday morning the skies looked different. High gray clouds covered the clear blue. The wind was blowing, though it carried no rain, but a feeling of something worse to come made Clari shudder. Miami was now under a hurricane watch. This meant the storm was likely to hit Miami within twenty-four hours. Hurricane Andrew would land on South Florida that night.

Clari followed Papi around the outside of the house as he and Mami covered the windows with sheets of plywood. It was a hard task. He drilled holes into the masonry around each window, placed lead anchors into the holes, and drove long, heavy screws into each. This way, the plywood was secured firmly against the masonry and would protect the glass from the wind or anything it flung.

Clari helped bring tools that Papi needed from the garage. At lunch time, Clari made sandwiches, but Papi and Mami were too busy to stop and eat. Clari brought their sandwiches and drinks outside and they took bites as they worked.

The house was getting darker as the light was blocked from each window. It was an odd thing, Clari thought, to come into her room in the middle of the day and have it be dark as night.

The neighbors were busy as well. Everyone hurried to protect their windows and bring in loose things from the yards. The air was filled with sounds of electric drills and saws. Even some ham-

mering could be heard. There were no children playing outside. Everyone was helping with prepara-
tions.

Clari was alone in the front yard when a white
van drove up. The passengers in it were elderly and
looked worried and sad. On the side of the van,
Clari read the sign, "Metro-Dade Transportation."
She remembered the announcements made on TV
for anyone who did not feel safe at home. A county
van would take them to a school used during the
storm as a shelter.

The van stopped in front of Mrs. Murphy's
house. Clari watched with surprise. She had
thought Mrs. Murphy was not worried about the
storm.

The driver, a tall black man, knocked on the
door. Mrs. Murphy came out, loaded down with bags
and packages in her arms. She carried her purse, a
travel bag, a pillow, and what looked like a plastic
bag full of family photos. In the other hand, she cradled Midnight and a bag of cat food.

"You can't bring pets to the shelter," the driver
shouted into the wind. He raised his hands and
waved them in warning.

"I've got to bring her! She'll be very quiet on my
lap!" Mrs. Murphy's cracking voice sounded like a
loud cry.

"I'm sorry. I'm not allowed to bring a pet in the
van. They won't allow her in the shelter, either.

Those are the rules," the man said, shaking his head.

"Oh, please." Mrs. Murphy seemed ready to cry. Clari felt sorry for her. "I can't leave her in the house alone!"

The man shook his head again. "Look, lady, we've got to go. I'll help you with your things while you put her back in the house."

The driver reached for the pillow in Mrs. Murphy's arm. Mrs. Murphy opened the door and leaned down to set Midnight inside, but the cat squirmed out of her hand and ran into the hedge on the side of the house.

"Oh, my!" Mrs. Murphy cried out, startled. "Come back here, Midnight! Come back, kitty!"

Mrs. Murphy ran after her cat. The bags and the purse that were looped around her arm flew off into the wind. Clari ran into her neighbor's yard and gathered the bags.

The driver went after Mrs. Murphy, who was kneeling down looking for Midnight. "We have to go! I have a few others to pick up still," the man shouted to make himself heard.

Mrs. Murphy nodded her head. The driver offered a hand to help her up from the ground. When she returned to the porch, her head and shoulders were hunched forward. She looked miserable. She locked the front door to her house and took the bags from Clari with a nod of gratitude.

Clari thought there was moisture filling the old lady's eyes.

"I'll find Midnight," Clari said to the old woman.

Mrs. Murphy's face brightened, but she didn't smile. "Thank you."

As the van drove away, Mrs. Murphy searched the bushes with her eyes. Clari watched her until the van disappeared around the corner, then she ran into her kitchen. It was dark and she had to turn on the lights to see. She found the bag of cat food that Mami had bought and ripped a hole in the top. Clari poured some of the dry bits of food into a red plastic bowl. When the food hit the bowl, it sounded like the corn cereal Clari ate for breakfast. But it smelled like sardines!

Clari ran out and called Midnight. "Here, kitty, kitty."

She reached the bushes where she had seen the cat disappear. The wind was beating the branches back and forth and rattling the leaves. Clari was sure Midnight was scared. She placed the bowl on the ground invitingly. But Midnight would not come out.

Clari got on her hands and knees and looked under the shrubs. She could see Midnight's bright, green eyes. Her black legs trembled. Midnight was scared of the wind.

"Come on out, Midnight. I just want to help you." Clari tried to say the words nicely, but she had to say them loud to be heard. Midnight didn't move.

Clari knew she should not reach in and grab her. A frightened animal can bite or scratch even when one is offering to help. Besides, she was wedged too deep in the hedge for Clari to reach.

Desperate, Clari took the bowl back to the kitchen. She poured the dry cat food back into the bag. From the fridge, she spooned some of the left-over *picadillo* into the bowl and put it in the microwave for a few seconds to warm it up. The heat released the aroma of the meat and Clari noticed she was getting hungry.

She returned with the bowl of meat and placed it in front of the bushes. "I have something special for you," Clari called to Midnight. "Come on, kitty. You can't stay outside in the hurricane."

Clari waited on her hands and knees again. After a moment, the black cat stepped out cautious-ly. She rubbed her silky warm side on Clari's arm and meowed. Then she licked the meat in the bowl.

When she finished the meat, Clari put her arms around Midnight. The cat purred happily against her chest. Clari picked up the empty bowl and hur-ried into the house.

She was relieved that Midnight would be safe, yet she didn't want her parents to know she had Mrs. Murphy's cat in the house. She had no idea what they would say. She only knew that she couldn't leave the helpless animal outside.

Once in her bedroom, she placed a furry bath mat under her bed and set Midnight on it.

"Be a good kitty. Don't make any noise. Don't let Mami and Papi know you're in my room. I'll keep you safe from the storm. But you must be quiet."

Midnight meowed. Clari smiled back. She closed the bedroom door and went to help her parents.

❧

By late afternoon, the wind had picked up. Strong gusts made walking against it hard. Now everyone shouted to be heard. The sky darkened and heavy gray clouds dropped sprinklings of rain. The wind swatted raindrops on Clari while she worked. This was no ordinary rainstorm.

"I'm glad we're almost finished," Mami shouted as the wind fought to pull her pretty hair out of the ponytail she wore.

"One more sheet of plywood and the house will be secure," Papi yelled.

"Do you think Mrs. Murphy will be all right? She's all alone in her house." Mami's face looked concerned.

"I don't know what to think. This is a strong hurricane."

"She's not home," Clari shouted over the wind. "Mrs. Murphy left!"

Her mother and father looked at her, surprised.

"Where did she go?" Papi asked. "She has no family here. Her children live up north."

"She went to a shelter," Clari shouted. "The county van took her awhile ago."

"I was going to ask her to spend the night in our house," Mami said.

Papi rolled his eyes. "I don't know which would have been worse: the hurricane, or the storm Mrs. Murphy would have raised inside our house!" Papi and Clari laughed.

"I have to start something for our dinner," Mami yelled. "I'll be back soon." Clari watched Mami walk against the wind with difficulty. She lifted each leg slowly, like a cartoon figure in slow motion.

"Come on, Clari," Papi called. "You and I have a job to do."

Clari followed him into the garage and took the tools he handed her. Papi carried the ladder under his arm. When they reached Mrs. Murphy's yard, Papi leaned the ladder against the house.

"What are you doing?" Clari shouted after him as Papi stepped up cautiously.

"I'm taking her TV antenna down," Papi yelled.

"But Mrs. Murphy said she didn't want you to do it!"

"I think she meant to say 'yes.'" Papi smiled and winked his eye.

The wind blew Papi's clothes tightly against his body in the front. In back, his shirt flapped loosely like a flying flag. Clari worried that the wind would blow him right off the roof. She held the ladder in place when it started shaking and threatening to fall off the side of the house.

In a few minutes, the antenna was loose. Papi eased it down by a cable attached to it, but the antenna swung in the fierce wind. Clari had to move out of the way. Finally, the antenna came to rest on the grass. Clari held down the ladder so Papi could make it down from the roof.

"You see, Clari, I think Mrs. Murphy is too stubborn to ask her neighbors for help!" Papi explained.

It took two trips to store the ladder and Mrs. Murphy's antenna in their garage. The gusts of wind made walking and carrying things very difficult. Their hair and tee-shirts were wet. A constant sprinkling of rain came down, almost horizontally, in the strong wind.

"We have to cut the last sheet of plywood into two pieces. One will be for the bathroom window, the other for the garage window," Papi said when Mami returned.

"I've been thinking," Mami said. Her eyes were soft and sad. "Those two are such small openings. Maybe we could use the wood for something else."

"There's no other glass in our house to cover," Papi said, puzzled.

"Yes, I know," Mami smiled shyly. "I was worried about Mrs. Murphy's picture window in the living room. She's so proud of it."

"Are you turning into a softie?" Papi asked her teasingly.

"I guess I am. Just like the softie who took down Mrs. Murphy's antenna." Mami pinched Papi's rib and he broke into laughter. Clari laughed at their silliness, too.

The three carried the large sheet of plywood to Mrs. Murphy's front yard. They fought the wind as if they were steering a sailboat in stormy seas. The wood would be large enough to cover the expensive glass and to protect the furniture inside from the wind and rain if the glass broke.

❧

It was dark outside when they finished squeezing the cars into the crowded garage and closed the door. The family was in for the night and for the duration of the hurricane. Papi turned on the TV to hear news of the storm's movement. He lined up flashlights and batteries, candles and Clari's radio on the coffee table.

Clari helped Mami clean the bathtub and disinfect it. Then, they filled it with fresh water.

"We won't drink the water from the tub," Mami said to Clari. "We'll use some of it for washing hands and faces, even for washing kitchen things. After a hurricane, the water could become muddy or might carry disease until the city workers can take care of it."

Clari heard Midnight calling from the bedroom, but Mami didn't hear the cat. There was so much noise coming through the window and from the running water filling the tub.

From there, she followed Mami into the kitchen. Clari was glad when they left the bathroom. It was the only room in the house where the howling of the wind against the uncovered glass made her shudder.

Mami put Clari to work saving ice cubes in plastic bags and refilling the ice trays. She also filled plastic soda bottles with water and set them in the freezer. Mami had already frozen five bottles. She said they would need them to keep the food cold if the hurricane cut off their electricity.

While her mother was busy fixing dinner, Clari took some cat food and a dish of water to her room. She had to sneak past Papi, but he was so busy putting batteries in her radio that he didn't see her.

Midnight purred happily in her arms. The black cat wasn't interested in the food, but she drank some water from the dish and returned to her temporary bed under Clari's bed.

"Eat every bite of food on the table," Mami told her family when she called them for dinner. She had served all kinds of dishes. "I don't want to keep leftovers in the refrigerator. We won't have a way to warm them up and the food will just spoil."

"Clari," Papi said with a sneaky wink of his eye. "Don't fill up. Later she'll want us to finish all the ice cream in the freezer and that'll be the best part."

Clari rubbed her hands together. "I'm beginning to like hurricanes."

"I'm afraid you won't feel the same after tonight." Papi was no longer smiling. "Hurricanes can't be taken lightly. This is a powerful one."

As the evening wore on, Clari could see the truth in her father's words. The wind howled ferociously. It puffed and pressed on the plywood covers like a giant wolf trying to blow the house down. They could hear things banging against the walls, and the cement tiles on the roof rattled. Kiki screeched in fear when an object hit the porch wall. They could see nothing outside. The only unprotected opening, the bathroom window, had frosted glass. Besides, it was very dark outside.

Mami set out a game of checkers. But no one could concentrate.

Every television station had stopped regular programs for the weekend. The local news and weather announcers had been giving information on the hurricane and how to protect homes and families. Clari and her parents watched nervously and took in all their advice.

The metal garage door banged and rattled loudly as a strong gust beat against it. Clari sat up, startled.

"I'm going to check the garage," Papi said, and headed to the kitchen.

Mami raced into the kitchen with Clari following closely behind. Clari wouldn't be left alone in any part of the house.

Mami blocked Papi's path to the garage. "I don't want you to open it," Mami said. "It's dangerous to go in there."

"The door is just rattling," Papi said calmly. "I want to see if I need to hammer a board to it to keep it from shaking."

With fear in her eyes, Mami let him through. Clari and Mami watched from the kitchen doorway. The wind blew through the cracks where the wide metal door met the door frame. Paper bags and other loose things stored in the garage flapped around the messy room. Papi's wavy hair was stirred by the drafts as he approached the door.

When the door banged loudly, Clari jumped back in fright. "Papi, come back!" she screamed. Kiki screeched in her towel-covered cage.

Papi returned to the kitchen and Mami locked the door behind him.

"It's secure," Papi said. "There's nothing I can do to keep it from shaking." Then, looking at his daughter's pale face, he put an arm around her shoulders. "There's something I can do to keep you from shaking."

He steered her to her room. "We're going to bring your mattress into the living room. It's the safest place in the house. You can sleep there while we watch TV."

Clari was grateful, though she knew she would not get any sleep tonight.

When they entered the room, she suddenly remembered Midnight. She had hidden Mrs. Murphy's cat carefully from her parents. Now the game was over. Midnight raced out from under the bed and caressed Clari's leg. She meowed, flashing her shiny green eyes.

Clari wondered what Papi would say. Clari was already restricted to her room as punishment, though no one seemed to remember.

"She's Mrs. Murphy's cat," Clari said, swallowing hard.

"I can see that," said Papi. He didn't sound too angry. "What I want to know is how she got in here."

"The man in the van wouldn't let Mrs. Murphy take Midnight with her."

"So she gave you her cat?" Papi asked, incredulous.

"No, Papi. She doesn't even know I have Midnight."

"She should have left the cat in her house. The cat would have been fine with a little food and water," Papi shook his head.

"That's what the man said. And Mrs. Murphy tried. But Midnight ran away when she opened the door to put her in the house." Clari looked at her father's face to determine if she was in trouble. But she only read surprise in his face. He was quietly watching the silky dark animal twine her way around Clari's leg.

After a while Clari said, "I guess you're mad at me. But don't be angry at Midnight. I'll keep her away from Kiki. I promise." Clari took Papi's hand in hers. "I just couldn't leave Midnight out in the storm. I have never seen Mrs. Murphy look so pitiful. I think she had tears in her eyes."

Papi looked at Clari and smiled. "We have another softie in the family," Papi announced, and he put his arms around Clari.

Fitting In

Clari lay on her mattress in the middle of the living room floor. She had been right. She would not get a wink of sleep tonight. Mami cuddled with her on the mattress and Papi stretched in his comfortable chair while they watched TV.

The news was frightening. The hurricane whipped up winds of great speed and power. The few cameramen risking their lives outside showed shots of tree branches and street signs flying end over end in the fierce wind and rain. The palms seemed to be bent over by the force of the wind. Traffic signals and street lights were out in many parts of the city. Not a person was seen on the streets, only the newsmen.

The loud rattling of the metal garage door had continued without stop. The wind beat ferociously at the house. It sounded like a locomotive coming at them at great speed. The cement tiles on the roof clattered like a thousand castanets. Papi feared they were losing some of them.

There was little for them to do but wait out the storm and eat. Earlier, Papi had dished out the most enormous ice cream sundaes Clari had ever seen. He had used up everything he could find in the refrigerator, three ice cream flavors, whipped topping, candy sprinkles, chocolate syrup, and spoonfuls of strawberry jam. He had enjoyed making them. Clari's sundae had been delicious. She thought she'd never eat again, she was so full.

Yet, when Mami announced a sudden desire for salty plantain chips and soda, Clari jumped right up and went to the kitchen with her.

"You read my mind," Clari said. "I'm in the mood for something salty now."

Midnight followed her in and wrapped herself around Clari's legs, meowing softly.

"I wonder what she thinks," Clari said, pouring out soda for the three of them. "Do cats understand what's going on outside?"

"I don't know." Mami stopped pouring out chips from the bag and looked down at Midnight. "I would think the noise is scary and confusing."

"She's been snuggling against me all night. I guess she can't sleep either."

"Neither can Kiki," Mami said, and crunched a chip with her teeth. "I covered his cage with a pillow case so he'd feel snug, but he calls out every few minutes."

"Maybe he's afraid of Midnight." Clari opened her mouth and ate the crunchy chips her mother placed in it.

"I don't think so." Mami tilted her head thoughtfully. "He might be confused. You know Kiki goes to sleep as soon as it's dark. Well, we darkened the house so early in the day, he doesn't know what to make of it."

Clari took a sip of her soda. The foamy bubbles clung to her lip like a golden mustache. "What about birds in the wild? Where do they go in a storm?"

"I imagine some fly to safer ground. Others find shelter in tree holes or low to the ground." Mami turned her head from side to side slowly. "I'm afraid many will not make it tonight."

Suddenly a tremendous crash, louder than anything they'd heard all night, pierced the calm interior of the house. The rooms were cast into total darkness. The TV died. Shattering glass tinkled and splintered as it hit hard surfaces. The fierce wind blasted through the rooms with a whistling roar. They were pelted with wet leaves and rain.

"Eeeeeh!" Clari pitched a high scream.

"Are you all right?" Papi yelled out his question. It was hard to hear over the roar of the wind.

"We're fine!" Mami shouted back. She hugged Clari to her tightly as they stood in place.

Clari saw the beam of Papi's flashlight. The beam was not coming closer to the kitchen. It was aimed away, toward the bedrooms.

"Papi, come back! Come rescue us!" Clari screamed.

"Stay where you are!" he yelled. "Don't come this way!"

"Papi will come back for us," Mami spoke in her ear. Clari's head rested on her mother's shoulder. "He has to check the damage."

The wind travelled through the dark house. It pelted them with rain as they stood in the kitchen.

"What do you think happened?" Clari asked, frightened.

"I don't know. I guess a window broke. I hope the plywood covers didn't give way." Mami held on to her and Clari was grateful to have someone to cling to in the darkness.

Now Clari and Mami saw the beam of light again heading back. Suddenly, the wind blowing inside the house stopped. But they heard a new rattling noise within the house. It seemed the hurricane wanted to be let in once more.

"What did you find? What broke?" Mami asked Papi anxiously.

"The window in the bathroom. Mrs. Murphy's grapefruit tree crashed against the house and broke through the window," Papi said, making his way to the kitchen.

"No!" shouted Mami in disbelief.

"Wow!" said Clari. "What's all that rattling we can hear now?"

"I've closed the bathroom door, but the wind blowing through the broken window is making the door shake. I have to find something in the garage to close up the opening."

"I'll get flashlights for Clari and me," Mami said, releasing her arms from around Clari.

"Don't leave me!" Clari cried.

In the darkness, Papi put his hand on Clari's shoulder. Clari felt reassured once again. "I'll stay here with you," said Papi. "I'll aim my light from here for Mami to find the other flashlights."

The garage was scarier than before. Clari and Mami lighted the path for Papi from the kitchen doorway. It was very dark. It seemed a monster gripped the metal door from outside and was trying to break it loose. The noise was ear-shattering. Clari wondered how long the wide garage door would hold up.

"Hurry up, Papi. This is too scary," she yelled out.

Papi returned with a hammer and nails, an old wood shelf board and pruning shears.

"What are you doing with those?" Mami asked, spotlighting the shears with the beam of her light.

"The bathroom is quite a sight. There are branches and twigs sticking through the window and silly green grapefruits dangling over the tub," Papi said. "I've got to cut the branches before I can cover the hole."

"I want to see the mess!" Clari blurted out.

Mami didn't like the idea. "It's too dangerous. The wind can blow something in and hurt us. And I'm sure there's glass all over the floor."

"It will be all right for a few minutes," Papi said. "You'll never see a bathroom like this again. Besides, I'm afraid I'm going to need your help."

When Papi opened the bathroom door, the wind pushed them back with force. But in single file, they slowly made it in. Clari searched with her flashlight. The sliding doors to the tub were shattered. Bits of glass were all over the floor. Grapefruit branches stuck through the bare opening where the glass window had been. They looked like skinny arms reaching into the house to get away from the storm. Baseball-sized fruit danced in clumps from the ends of branches shuddering in the wind.

The clean water Mami and Clari had put in the tub was no longer clear. Fruit, torn green leaves and sticks had fallen into it. In the bottom of the white tub, Clari could see the shattered remains of the glass window. Their supply of clean water was ruined.

"So much for washing ourselves in the next few days." Mami looked disappointed, though she managed a smile.

Papi got to work. Mami aimed the beam of her flashlight on his hands. He reached over the full tub and cut twigs and sticks, dropping them into the water without regard. He had to work fast.

The wind was whipping everything in the room. Clari gathered the soaked towels, which flapped on their racks as if they had life. She threw them in a corner of the kitchen and raced back. She'd rather be in the windy bathroom than alone in the dark, noisy house.

Mami helped Papi hold the board in place. It was Clari's job this time to aim her flashlight on the work area. They fought the strong wind while Papi hammered nails into the wall. The first nails gave way, sending the board swinging under Mami's hands. For a moment, everyone held his breath. But Papi pushed the board against the opening again and hammered long nails all around until his hands turned white from the effort. Finally, he had the wind under control, at least inside the house.

"We did it!" said Papi, and he gave them a thumbs-up signal under Clari's light. They laughed with relief.

"Let's get out of here and close the door quickly!" said Mami, leading Clari out of the bathroom.

"Don't you trust my work?" Papi teased Mami. But he followed the two into the hallway and closed the door behind him.

❧

The winds died down slowly. Clari could tell by the quieting of the doors and roof tiles. After a while, there was little noise coming from the roof and only occasional clattering from the doors as gusts of wind threw final dying punches. There had been no other way to tell the hurricane had passed, as the interior of the house was as dark now as it had been all night.

Papi's watch told them it was eight-thirty in the morning. She had never spent a night like this before. She had not slept a wink. She hadn't even tried, though she admitted to herself she'd been too scared to close her eyes. The wonder was that she was not tired now. She was ready to go out and explore the neighborhood.

"Put sturdy shoes on and come out with me," Papi said when she asked if they could.

"I can't wait to see Mrs. Murphy's tree!" Clari said, lacing up her sneakers hurriedly.

"I want to see what the hurricane did to our roof." said Papi.

The sight that greeted them when Papi opened the front door amazed them. Every part of the yard, the sidewalk, and the street was covered with roof tiles, wrinkled aluminum sheets, tree branches and leaves, wood pieces, cardboard, paper, and items Clari didn't recognize. Many things had come from far away. Everything was damp, though there was no flooding, as Clari had expected. There were hardly even any puddles.

The neighbors were coming out of their homes to inspect the damage. They looked around, dazed by the mess. None of the homes had electricity or phone service. The tiles of most roofs had been ripped off by the wind. The glass panes on many of the unprotected windows had broken, leaving the rooms soggy and the furniture destroyed.

"We'll have to get a new roof," Papi said, looking up. "It's down to the tar paper."

"Do you think it will leak?" Mami asked with a worried look on her face.

"I don't know." Papi shrugged. "I'll climb up on it later and see if I can make repairs until a roofer can come out."

Clari couldn't believe the force of the wind. Cement tiles were so heavy to lift! Yet they'd been blown off the roof and across the lawn. Cars that had not been stored in garages during the hurricane were dented, their windows crushed. There were large branches torn from trees. Two houses down, a neighbor's large mango tree was lying on the ground. Its roots were turned up, bare of soil. As she looked down the street, Clari noticed many other trees knocked down by the power of the wind.

Clari ran to the side of the house to see Mrs. Murphy's grapefruit tree. "Papi, come and see!" Clari yelled.

The tree had been pushed down onto the Martínez's house. Its canopy, like an open umbrella, pressed onto their wall and onto the place where the bathroom window had been.

"It took the fence with it!" said Mami when she arrived at the spot.

"That can be fixed," Papi said. "It broke the horizontal bar at the top of the fence and the weight of the tree bent the fence."

"What a shame. Mrs. Murphy loved this tree."

"I guess my pruning job didn't keep the tree from getting knocked down," Papi teased.

Mami smiled. "I guess not."

"What a mess! We can't even eat all this green fruit!" said Clari. She hopped over the trunk to the other side of the tree. "What are these wires?"

Papi looked where she pointed. Electric and telephone wires lay on the ground, pinned by the tree. The wires were attached to the pole at the back corner of their house.

"Stay away from those!" Papi and Mami yelled as one.

"They could be live power lines. Get back on this side of the tree right away," Papi said. Clari knew by her parents' reaction that this was serious business.

"Looks like the tree ripped down our electric and phone lines," Papi said, helping her back over the trunk. "We might be without service for a long time."

"Mrs. Murphy's house seems fine," Mami said, waving them over to walk around the neighbor's yard. "Some of the roof tiles are missing, but the windows didn't break."

"Some luck! Here I covered all our windows but two and we get a broken window. Hers were not protected and her house did fine."

"Mrs. Murphy *is* lucky! She's lucky to have a neighbor like you. Come look at this." Mami led Papi by the hand as they walked toward Mrs. Murphy's front yard.

A wrinkled aluminum sheet lay on her lawn. It looked like part of a neighbor's tool shed. It came to rest a few feet away from the plywood-covered picture window.

"The plywood has a deep scratch. I think the piece of aluminum was hurled into it by the wind." Papi examined the wood closely.

"I think so, too." Mami looked from the covered window to the big metal sheet on the ground. "It would have shattered her beautiful picture window."

"It would have been the end of her living room." Clari had a scary thought. "What if Midnight had been inside by herself?"

Mami nodded. A thoughtful look lingered on her face. "Mrs. Murphy could have been in there alone, too."

Papi started to walk back to their home. "Come on, *mi hija*. We have a big clean-up job ahead of us."

After eating a quick, cold breakfast, the neighbors got together to pick up the trash on the street. They piled it in mounds on the grassy swales in front of each property. When they finished, the families began the great task of cleaning up their houses and yards. It would take weeks, everyone agreed.

Papi removed some of the wood covering their windows and offered it to neighbors who had lost windows and had no way to cover them now. None of the stores had opened. Some were destroyed. There was no way to buy building supplies.

When the electric power was restored to the block, there was a moment of triumph. Neighbors carried the news happily up the street. Families ran in and out of their houses to test the lights.

Clari left her work and sprinted into their home hoping they, too, had somehow gotten power. But there was no good news when she switched each knob. She couldn't hear the welcome hum of the fridge coming back to life. Papi had been right, the tree had cut their power off.

Mami and Clari worked all day alongside Papi, but there was so much to do that by late afternoon, their yard still looked messy.

They paused from the work and stared tiredly at the Metro-Dade van that drove slowly up the street. Clari noticed the driver was different. This time it was a woman. But she still recognized one of the van's elderly passengers. Mrs. Murphy looked tired and sad as she looked at her home with big, round eyes.

The van stopped, and she came out with the help of the driver. Mrs. Murphy carried the things she had taken to the shelter under her arms. She stood on the grass facing her house.

Her mouth opened in surprise. She stared at the covered picture window and the big aluminum sheet that lay at her feet.

Mrs. Murphy walked into her house and came back out shortly, empty-handed. Clari and her family watched again as she inspected the downed grapefruit tree. Mrs. Murphy shook her head. Then, the old woman crossed the yard and approached Clari's parents.

"You put up the wood cover on my window, didn't you? I am deeply grateful. My house would have been destroyed."

Papi smiled.

"He used our last piece. It was supposed to cover our bathroom window," Clari piped up. Embarrassed, Mami and Papi hushed her.

"Oh, my!" Mrs. Murphy exclaimed. "And my tree broke your window! I'm so sorry."

"And took our electric and phone lines with it!"

"Clari!" Mami gave her an annoyed look.

Clari shrugged her shoulders. "She's going to find out anyway."

"It's not your fault, Mrs. Murphy," Papi said. "If it is going to happen, it will happen."

"And it ruined the water in our tub, too!"

"Clarita! That's enough! Go in the house right now!" he yelled in Spanish. Papi's eyebrows joined above his nose. She knew she had crossed the line again.

Clari walked to the front door. When she turned and saw the sad look in Mrs. Murphy's eyes, she regretted being so mean. Clari stopped on the porch and listened as Mrs. Murphy continued.

"I was a long time in the van. We took other people home first. The driver had to find ways around all the obstacles on the road."

"The neighbors say all the traffic signals are out," Papi told her.

"Not one is working. Drivers have to take turns to cross each street. It takes forever," said Mrs. Murphy.

Mami nodded her head. "A very strong hurricane."

Suddenly, Clari remembered Midnight. She was sure Mrs. Murphy would be delighted to see that her cat was unhurt. Maybe Clari could make up for her meanness by showing her Midnight was safe.

"There's so much damage all around. I was worried about my house," Mrs. Murphy was saying when Clari returned to the porch with the silky black cat in her arms.

"I look at your roof when I climb up on mine today. Some tiles are gone, but no more problems," Papi assured the widow.

"I'm really sad about my cat, Midnight. She ran away from me yesterday. I'm afraid I won't see her again."

"Oh, yes you will. I've got her right here," Clari said.

Mrs. Murphy was stunned. "My kitty! You found her!" her voice cracked with emotion.

Clari handed her the warm furry creature. Mrs. Murphy rubbed the silky bright face on her cheek. Midnight meowed contentedly.

"Clari took Midnight into our house before the hurricane. She put her in her bedroom," Mami said, putting an arm around Clari.

Mrs. Murphy's lips curved in a bright, grateful smile. Clari thought this was the first time she had seen Mrs. Murphy happy.

"Thank you, Clari," the old woman said. Clari was surprised. She didn't think Mrs. Murphy knew her name.

Then Mrs. Murphy turned to Clari's parents and said, "Thank you."

❧

After dark, Papi heard a weak tapping at the front door. Holding a flashlight to show him the way, he opened it. There stood Mrs. Murphy with a steaming bowl of spaghetti and meat sauce. She had wrapped a loaf of Italian bread in foil and held it balanced on top of the bowl.

"I brought a warm dinner for the three of you," Mrs. Murphy said. Her smile pulled the aged lines of her face into happy angles. "I hope Clari likes spaghetti and garlic bread." The old lady looked at Clari and winked a cheerful eye at her.

Clari's mouth watered from the wonderful smell filling the house.

"Thank you. I was going to make cold sandwiches tonight," Mami said, taking the warm bowl from her. "This is very nice of you, Mrs. Murphy."

"Please call me Adele, dear."

"Thank you, Adele," said Mami, exchanging surprised glances with Papi.

"My fridge is working, dear," the old woman continued. "I would be happy to put your food in it. I can take some back with me right now."

"Thank you. I will check to see what can be saved," Mami said, leading her into the kitchen. Glowing candles provided the only light in the house.

"Clari," Mrs. Murphy said, turning to the young girl. Clari was amazed at the change in Mrs. Murphy. She didn't know what to expect next. "If you'd like, you can go home with me and bring back a bucket of water for your use."

Clari's mouth dropped open. All she could do was nod.

"That will help very much," said Papi, who had followed the women into the kitchen. He signalled Clari and she ran into the garage. With the help of a flashlight, she soon found a clean bucket and hurried back.

In the kitchen, Papi, Mami, and Mrs. Murphy sorted through the food which now was stored in the picnic cooler with ice. They filled a grocery bag with the things that required cooking and would soon spoil.

"I help you carry this," Papi said, lifting the bag.

Mrs. Murphy turned to Mami as they headed out. "I want you to cook your meals at my house until your electricity is back."

"That's all right, Mrs. Murphy. I mean, Adele," Mami said, and smiled. "My husband will light the barbecue every day. I will cook on it."

"I will bring you coffee in the morning," she said, walking to the door. Then Mrs. Murphy turned to Papi, as if she had remembered something important. "Oh, Mr. Martínez. About the fence..."

Papi interrupted her. "Don't worry, I cut down the tree and I fix it."

"Oh, no. That's not what I meant." Mrs. Murphy stopped and shook her head. "I was talking about the back, where my yard meets the park."

Clari knew just where she meant. She was talking about the place where Clari climbed over. Clari looked down, ashamed.

"I wonder if you can help me install a gate for Clari." Mrs. Murphy smiled back when Clari stole a glance at her. "It's a long walk around the block for such a nice girl."

A Do-It-Yourself Project

Mari had never heard that word before! Not in all of her thirteen years. It wasn't because English was her second language. Speaking with a Spanish accent didn't mean she couldn't understand.

Besides, as she looked around the classroom, she could tell many of the kids were just as puzzled as she was. And their only language *was* English. Robbie's mouth opened wide, like a frog's catching a fly. The two girls who were always together, Erica and Cathy, asked each other, "What?" their eyebrows arched up in question.

"DIORAMA," Mrs. Graham had said. "You must make a diorama. It should show the food chain of life in Biscayne Bay."

Only the smart kid, Jake, seemed to know what the word meant. He glanced at everybody through his wire-rimmed glasses. His lips curved with the subtle smile he used at times like this. *I know what she means and you don't*, it seemed to say.

"Your projects will be judged and ribbons will be awarded to those that best show what we've been studying in class," Mrs. Graham said. "The dioramas are due in two weeks."

Two weeks! She needed that much time to find out what the word meant! Mari looped a strand of her long, black hair around a finger and looked around the room again. She hoped someone other than Jake appeared confident. Then, maybe, she would ask that person after class. But not arrogant Jake; he'd be the last one she'd go to for help. No one else had a relaxed look. Some jotted down the word in their notebooks so it wouldn't escape them. Mari did the same. Perhaps the other students would get help from their moms and dads and have them solve the mystery.

Liz, sitting in the third row, raised her hand. If she asked the question that silently hovered above every kid's puzzled head, Mrs. Graham would put her in her place. Laughter from the class would be sure to follow.

Mrs. Graham's assignments were never questioned. One either understood what she meant or found out on one's own. Mrs. Graham assumed everyone loved natural science as well as she did. Every kid in her class knew that she lived what she taught. Mari figured her home was landscaped to represent the habitats she described in class. She probably had an arid desert, a tropical jungle, a seaside garden. Maybe she lived by the ocean.

All eyes were on Liz, the dark-haired girl. Her hand had been up, patiently waiting for permission to speak.

"Yes?" Mrs. Graham stretched out the word, as though the three letters had multiple syllables.

"What is a diorama?" The girl gulped silently.

It took courage, Mari knew. The students were quiet. She was sure they held back the laughter because it could have been any one of them asking the same question.

"Look it up!" Mrs. Graham answered. The class laughed, but this time it was a nervous kind of giggle, as if to conceal that they were as guilty as Liz. "You're in the eighth grade. You must do your own thinking. If I tell you all the answers, they won't stick."

Mari was worried. She wanted to do well in this class. She even liked nature and things having to do with it. She should have known that Mrs. Graham would leave it up to them.

"Please remember," Mrs. Graham said as the bell rang and the students gathered their books, "this is supposed to be fun. I'm sure you'll have a great time making your dioramas."

Fun? How could school work possibly be fun? Mrs. Graham, Mari thought, was a strange woman.

❧

It was after dinner before Mari got around to thinking about the assignment. She had done her math homework while watching reruns of her favorite shows on TV. She had found time to talk on the phone to her friend Ana and even listened to the radio. That always put her in a good mood.

When her mother got home from work, they ate together. Mari washed the dishes every evening. She could think of many other things she'd rather do instead of dishes, but Mamá was right. She had to help. At least, since there were just two of them, there were only two plates, two glasses, two forks, and two knives. She dunked each pair in the soapy water, rinsed them, and placed them on the drying rack. Like Noah's ark, two of each kind, except she plunged them into the flood waters before they were allowed into the ark.

The thought came to her while soaking the sauce pan covered with a creamy layer of red kidney-bean soup, and while scraping the crusty frying pan in which Mamá had browned the bread-ed fish steaks Mari had so enjoyed. It might have been triggered by the salty, fishy smell that rose up above the sink as she filled the pan with suds. In any case, she remembered the ocean, which brought to mind the bay and the creatures that lived there. She was reminded of the food chain which she had to show in a.... What was that word again? She could not think of it. She was glad she had written it down.

When the dishes were dried and put away, she went to her room and looked up the word. DIORA-MA. She'd have to remember that. Now, to figure out what it meant, she'd look it up in her dictionary.

Di-no-saur; *dip*. The word belonged between these two. She was sure. But it wasn't listed in her dictionary. She knew she had not misspelled it. She had copied it carefully from the board, where Mrs. Graham had taken the time to write it out for the class.

Mamá had given Mari the dictionary a few years ago, when they'd arrived from Cuba and Mari was learning English. It had helped her a lot back then. She could understand the meaning of the words by the colorful pictures that went with them. Mari knew she had outgrown the small book. She would be embarrassed to admit to her friends that she used a children's dictionary. But it was the only one they had at home.

"Mamá," Mari called in Spanish. "Where are you?"

"I'm heading out to do the laundry," Mamá answered her in Spanish, the language they spoke when they were together. She carried a plastic basket loaded with dirty clothes.

"I need your help with a school project." Mari held open the door to their apartment to let her mother through.

"You'll have to come with me to tell me about it. I've got to get this started." Mamá locked the door behind them. "Help me carry the detergent."

Mari followed her mother a few doors down to the laundry room. It was always warm and humid in the small room, in spite of the fresh breeze coming through the window. Light tufts of fuzz clung to the unpainted concrete walls. Thankfully, the banged-up washer and drier were free. Mamá sorted their clothes into two piles, then started to fill the washer.

"I have to find out what a 'diorama' is." Mari pronounced the odd word in English.

Mamá looked up. Her brown eyes, as shiny and dark as her daughter's, were wide open. "A what?"

"A 'diorama.' You have to explain to me what it is so I can make one."

"*Mi amor*, I have never heard the word before in Spanish or in English." Mamá continued to fill the washer with clothes.

Mari didn't like it when her mother called her *mi amor*, my love. Mari knew she was Mamá's only love now. "Well, what am I going to do? I don't know what the teacher wants."

"Have you looked up the word in the dictionary?" Mamá said without stopping her work.

Mari pressed her lips together and sighed. She didn't want to hurt Mamá's feelings, but it was time she knew Mari's dictionary wasn't useful anymore. "That dictionary is for young children. It isn't any good for me."

Mamá's brows came together above her nose. "It may have pictures in it for children, but the explanations are useful, even for me. I bought it when we had very little money to spare for things like books," Mamá reminded her.

"I'm not saying I'm not grateful, Mamá. It was great when I was learning English."

She hated when her mother made her feel guilty. Especially when Mamá was missing the point. Mari was too old now for that book. "Children don't need to look up that many words. It's too small for me now. Anyway, the word 'diorama' is not in it."

Mamá placed two quarters in the slots and shoved the money tray into the box at the top of the washer. With loud clicking and jerking, the machine came to life and water began pouring into the tub. Mamá let the water run over the back of her hand to test it for warmth.

"It's supposed to be about the food chain in the bay," Mari said when her mother didn't offer any other help. She tried to use the right words in Spanish to explain something she had heard of only in English.

"She wants you to make a chain out of vegetables?" Mamá's puzzled face had a faraway look, like she had many other things on her mind.

"No, not a chain made out of food!" Mari said, starting to lose her patience. "The food chain has to do with big fish eating little fish, things like that." How could she get any help if she first had to teach her mother what the project was all about? "I just don't know what the teacher wants us to do."

"*Mi amor*, you are in her classroom and I'm not. How would I know what your teacher wants?" Mamá said without looking up.

Mari shrugged her shoulders. She tested her mother. "I guess I can't do the project."

"I won't accept your giving up." Mamá gave her a serious look. "You can ask your teacher or a friend in the class. Go to the library after school tomorrow and find out what that strange word means."

"Papá would know," Mari grumbled just loud enough for her mother to hear. "If he were still here, he'd help me."

Mamá measured out the powdered detergent slowly, glancing at Mari from the corner of her eye. Her face was not happy. "Mari, Papá doesn't live with us anymore. You must figure out problems by yourself." Pouring the snowy powder into the water, Mamá shrugged her shoulders and continued, "I doubt he would understand all these new scientific things you're studying, anyway."

Mari stomped out of the laundry room and headed back to the apartment. With her arms crossed over her chest, she waited for her mother to unlock the door. Mamá was wrong. If Papá were here, he would help her like he had helped her with math before. But Papá had been gone for a few months. He and Mamá were divorced. He had moved from Miami to New York City, where he hoped to find better work. Though at first Mari had hoped he would return to them, she was now convinced he had moved out for good. Still, she never lost a chance to remind her mother how angry and hurt she was over it.

Mamá just didn't have the answers. She hadn't studied these things in her time, and hardly knew the language of their new country. Besides, Mamá worked many hours as a cashier at the supermarket and had to keep up with the chores when she got home. Since Papá left, Mamá had little time to spend with Mari.

While she hated to admit it, Mari knew she had to do what Mamá suggested. She'd have to find a way on her own.

She'd ask what other kids were doing and maybe even go to the library after school. But she wouldn't ask Jake. And she wouldn't ask Mrs. Graham, either. She knew better.

❦

The next day, Mari had a chance to visit the
library during her English class. Her English
teacher usually let four students go to the library
during the last fifteen minutes of class. There, she
opened a heavy dictionary and searched under 'D.'

"*di-o-ram-a: noun. A scene reproduced in three
dimensions by placing objects, figures, etc. in front of
a painted background.*"

Finally, she had an answer! Mrs. Graham wanted them to make a miniature scene of the life of the
bay. She had to show how each living thing was
dependent on another for food by making little models of them. After all the worry, Mari felt a flood of
relief. But the work was still ahead. Now, she had to
decide how she would do it. She had never seen a
diorama before.

When she got up to put the dictionary away,
Mrs. Frank, the librarian, asked if Mari needed
help. Mari had always turned down her sweet
offers, but this time she said yes.

"I have to make a diorama for my Natural Science class," Mari told her. "I have never made one. I
have never even seen one," she laughed nervously.

"I have photographs of some that students
made in years before. Would you like to see them?"
Mrs. Frank led her to her office and took five pictures from her desk drawer.

They were beautiful small scenes of landscapes. One showed a river with a cow pasture on one side and a sugar cane field on the other. The river flowed into a marshy area in which the plants were shown to be dying. A girl glowing with pride and holding a red ribbon stood by the project. In another photo, a pimply-faced boy held a diorama of sand dunes with sea oats growing on them. The ocean was made out of clear dark-blue cellophane. Each project had won a ribbon.

"I'd like to show you my favorite one," said Mrs. Frank. She opened the door to a storage case. "This scene shows the daily life of the Seminoles living in the Everglades." Mrs. Frank brought the diorama out and set it on a table. "I like it very much because it was made with natural materials."

On a sandy island in the middle of the box, there was a small *chickee* hut, the palm-frond house used by the Native American tribe of South Florida. It was made out of reeds and grasses. A tiny wooden canoe, resembling the kind the Seminoles carved from a single log, rested on the painted water. Straw dolls were dressed in colorful calico clothes Seminole women take pride in making.

"The student made the dolls, too?" Mari asked, amazed.

"No, I think he bought them at a souvenir shop. But he made everything else. He even carved the canoe." Mrs. Frank ran a finger down the side of the rough, miniature boat.

"It's beautiful!" Mari exclaimed. "What kind of box did he use?" She walked around the table to view the back of the four-sided stage.

"Just about any grocery-store carton would do. You can cut out the top and one side and paint a background scene on the in—" The loud sound of the bell interrupted Mrs. Frank's words. She didn't fight the ringing. She waited quietly for it to end. "What is your topic?"

"The food chain in Biscayne Bay," Mari said. She anxiously glanced at the other students, who picked up their books and were moving on to other classes.

"Would you like me to find some books on the subject? I can have them ready for you after school," Mrs. Frank asked, realizing Mari had to go.

"Yes, that would really help me." Mari thanked her and ran out of the library.

❧

Sitting on her bed that afternoon, Mari leafed through the three books Mrs. Frank had selected for her. One was a biology book which had a chapter on food chains. Another was a book on marine life of southern Florida. The third book showed examples of three-dimensional models and directions for making them. Mari's mind raced with ideas on how to design her project. She could buy crinkly cellophane for the light-green water of the bay. And she'd get the beautiful, shiny fish she'd seen at the museum store when they took a school trip. The handmade fish were expensive, but now she had a valid reason to buy them.

When she heard the jingle of Mamá's keys in the door, Mari ran to the living room to greet her.

"Mamá, I have some great ideas for my project!" Mari said excitedly in Spanish.

Mamá nodded. She looked tired. "I'm glad to hear it," she said.

"I'm going to need your help for a few things. Can you bring a couple of empty boxes from work tomorrow? They should be this big," said Mari, measuring an imaginary square with her hands.

"Sure. I can do that," Mamá said, walking into the kitchen.

Mari followed. "You have to give me some money to buy supplies. I know just what I want."

Mamá dried her freshly washed hands on the apron she had tied around her waist. "I don't have any money." She looked at Mari, without a smile to soften her tired eyes. "The check from Papá has not arrived this month, and I still have to pay the rent."

Mari was disappointed. She knew this was a point she could not argue and expect to win. Papá sent them small amounts of money, but he wasn't always on time. After paying bills, Mamá was usually short of cash for the rest of the month.

While Mamá cooked dinner, Mari set the table for the two of them. Then Mari returned to her room and plopped down on the bed. So much for using cellophane and expensive, hand-painted museum fish! She'd have to find a different way.

She thought about Mrs. Frank's comment on using natural products. It wouldn't cost much if she found the things around the neighborhood. Finding and gathering them would be fun. Using sand on the floor of the box, she could represent the bottom of the sea. If only she could get to the beach. A little combing of the beach would give her lots of material to make her work look realistic.

She opened the book on making models and browsed through it. A section of the book had instructions for making figures out of homemade clay. A portion of flour, a portion of salt, and a little water made a molding dough. Perhaps she could use this dough to shape sea creatures. She had all the ingredients at home. But she would still need paint for the animals and for the background. And this would require money.

Breaking the silence at dinner, Mari brought up the diorama again. "I need you to take me to the beach. Can we go this weekend?"

"*Mi amor*, I work six days a week. How can I spend my only day off at the beach?" Mamá looked at her lovingly, but her eyes were droopy. Mari knew she was tired.

"But Mamá, I need to collect a few things for my project. It won't cost us a thing. And you can help me. It will be fun!"

"Oh, Mari," was all Mamá said as she took another bite of *bistec*, the thin Cuban steak smothered with fried onions. From her tone, Mari knew Mamá was softening.

"We could find some sand for the bottom and some shells, and seaweed, and twigs… I promise we can go home right after." She gave her mother an orphaned-puppy-dog look that said, *Take pity on me.* "You told me to figure out a way on my own."

Mamá smiled. "Very well. We'll take a little time Sunday afternoon."

"There is one thing I will still need to buy. Poster paints," Mari said, breaking a small piece of crusty Cuban bread. "They sell them at your store. They're not that much money and with your discount…"

Mamá nodded her head and smiled. Mari could tell she was giving in to her request. "There's four dollars in my wallet. You can have three. Meet me at the store tomorrow and we'll see what you need."

The diorama was taking shape. The store manager where Mamá worked had given Mari a sturdy carton that had held boxed cookies. He even helped her cut off the sides she didn't need.

Mari was pleased with the paints she'd bought. Although only four colors had been in the package, Mari had a knack for mixing them to get all the shades she wanted. She painted a background divided horizontally into sky, water surface, and underwater levels. Using different shades of soft blue and clear light green, it was easy to tell the sea apart from the sky with its puffy, white clouds.

The trip to the beach had been a success. Mari found many colorful shells and cut small bits of sea grass and weeds that had dried up above the surf line. Mari's enthusiasm spilled over to Mamá, who kept her eyes lowered to the sandy beach looking for useful things. Mamá discovered small bits of coral and sponges that had washed up on shore. She handed Mari a large paper cup to bring back sand. Mari was glad Mamá had taken the time to go to the beach and relax. She could tell Mamá had a good time.

Maybe Mrs. Graham was right after all. Making a diorama was turning out to be fun!

After school, she opened her locker and decided which books she would need for homework. As she filled her backpack, Erica and Cathy, the two girls from Natural Science class, came up to their lockers.

"My diorama is looking great!" Cathy said. "We used iridescent paper to show the water and plaster to make the shore. Wait till you see it!"

"My dad is helping me," Erica said. "He takes an underwater camera when he goes diving. He gave me great pictures to use as our background. Maybe I should say I'm helping him!"

Great! Mari thought. Erica is getting help from her father. Her diorama will look perfect, like an adult worked on it. She continued to listen, pretending to be busily sorting through the junk in her locker.

"My dad built a wooden box to display my diorama," said Jake, the smart kid, who had now joined them at the wall of lockers. "He's really handy and has lots of ideas for it. I guess our project will be very scientific."

"Well, my mom is an artist. She's giving me a hand, too," Cathy told them. "If she weren't, my diorama would look awful! I'm not handy at all."

It seemed like everyone's parents were getting in on the act. It wasn't fair. Mari had no one to help her make hers.

"No, I'm not artistic either," Erica told Cathy. "Mine would look homemade without my dad's help. I'd probably just have sand and a few shells."

Mari was devastated. Hers looked homemade! It was decorated with sand and a few shells, just as Cathy had said.

"How's yours coming along, Mari?" Erica asked, turning to her.

The question took Mari by surprise. She had fallen deep into her sad thoughts, regretting her choice of materials and angry that her father was not around to help her.

"Have you started working on it?" Jake asked her.

"Yes. I've been working on it. It's coming along fine," Mari said, her Spanish accent coming through her words and annoying her. She padlocked the door to her locker and picked up her backpack. "I've got to go now."

❧

The school library was almost empty after class the next day. Shyly, Mari approached Mrs. Frank. The librarian put her book down and looked up at her over her reading glasses.

"Hello, Mari. Did you find the books useful?" she asked, smiling sweetly.

"Yes. Thank you. I'm finished with them now." Although Mari was grateful, she could not bring herself to smile. She was too disappointed in her work.

"What did you decide to do about your diorama?" Mrs. Frank questioned her with interest.

"I'm using things found in nature, like you said." Mari saw Mrs. Frank's face light up. But Mari didn't think she had cause to feel proud.

"That sounds like an excellent choice," Mrs. Frank said.

"Well, I'm afraid it wasn't." Mari hung her head. "All the other kids have their parents helping them. My mother can't help me. She hardly speaks English and doesn't understand what the teacher wants. My father moved away. My diorama will look like a kindergartner made it!"

Mrs. Frank removed her glasses and set them on her desk. She took her time to speak, and for a moment Mari thought she had nothing to say. Then the soft-spoken librarian asked, "Why don't you tell me what materials you used?"

"I got beach sand for the bottom of the bay and scattered a few shells and bits of coral in it." Mari examined her fingernails nervously. "To make it look realistic, I put dried sea grass growing from the bottom of the sea. I found some twigs, that I glued to the shallow end, to represent red mangrove. The roots reach into the salt water. I cut tiny leaves from bits of green gift wrap and glued them to the tops of the twigs."

"So far, it sounds wonderful!" said Mrs. Frank.

"I know, but the others are using fancy paints and pictures, and even special wooden boxes instead of grocery-store cartons. My mom says we don't have money to spare for such things."

"Well, it doesn't matter what you use. The teacher will be looking for the amount of care each student puts into her work," Mrs. Frank said, looking into Mari's sad, brown eyes. "What are you using for the animals?"

Mari reached in her book bag and pulled out a small box held together with a rubber band. She opened it and took out a cotton-wrapped figure. It was a little, white fish, unpainted and delicate.

"I made these out of dough, from the recipe in the book you gave me." Mari watched Mrs. Frank for a reaction to her work.

Mrs. Frank took the little fish in her hand gently. She put her reading glasses back on and examined it. "Why, you've carved out little circles for the eyes and tiny half moons for scales. You've even scraped little lines down the length of the fins," Mrs. Frank said, clearly impressed.

Mari smiled. "I used a pin from my mother's sewing basket and carved out the lines and curves while the dough was soft." She removed the cotton from a few other figures and set each one on Mrs. Frank's desk.

"Let's see. You've made bigger fish and a tiny crab." The librarian looked the dough figures over carefully.

"Well, the little crab has no legs yet," Mari said, laughing at the little white shell in Mrs. Frank's hand. "I'm going to make them out of soft, thin wire that I found among my dad's tools. I might even paint it with pink nail polish."

Mrs. Frank nodded her head and smiled. "And this bird is beautiful!" She pointed to the spread wings, too afraid to take the delicate figure in her hand.

"That's an osprey," said Mari proudly. "They hunt for fish as they fly above the bay. I left a ceiling on my display box so I could hang a bird from it."

Mrs. Frank shook her head with disbelief. "Your work is wonderful!"

Mari thanked her. She raised her shoulders, still unsure of herself. "Well, I still have to paint the animals. I hope they look as realistic when I finish."

Mrs. Frank opened her desk drawer. She took out a small bottle and handed it to Mari. "See if you'd like to put glitter on the sides of the fish. It will make them look like the summer sun is reflecting off their scales."

"Thank you. This is great!" Mari shook the silver dust happily. "Maybe I can mix it with the paint I use."

Mrs. Frank helped her wrap the dough creatures back in their protective cotton coats. "You
know, Mari," the librarian said, "I wouldn't worry
about the work the other students are doing. It
seems to me, you're doing a great job all by yourself."

∾

Soon, the big day arrived. Mrs. Graham and
Mrs. Frank had arranged tables in the library into a
large rectangle. The students brought their projects
in the morning and set them up for the judges. They
would go to classes and return later in the day, after
the dioramas had been examined and judged.

Mari looked around the room. Everyone had a
different way of representing the same idea: the
food cycle of the creatures of Biscayne Bay. She was
amazed at the variety of materials selected to build
the models. Some used bright, shiny paints and glittery, shredded tissue paper. One student used fabric
with a beach scene as a background. Mari thought
she even detected a fishy smell coming from one of
the dioramas. One diorama was lighted with a black
light which made the bottom of the ocean and the
creatures in it glow. Many had the sharp polish of
an adult behind all the fine work.

One of the students had used the pretty museum fish Mari had liked. Mari was sorry she had not

been able to make her diorama as pretty as this one was.

Mari knew her project was not going to impress the other students. Even so, she was proud of all the effort she had put into it. It looked like a real bay scene. Three glittery fish chased each other with open mouths by order of their size. She'd elevated the fish above the sandy bottom with small sections of clear drinking straws. But, the smallest of the three was held up by the spring of a ball-point pen. The littlest fish bounced at the slightest touch, as though it were attempting to jump out of the water to capture the tiny pink crab. The shiny, polished crab rested on a leggy mangrove root, peacefully eating a rotting leaf. Above it were the remains of the osprey's last meal, a small dead fish whose white bones showed through, dangling from the mangrove branches. The bird flew against the sky of the diorama, suspended by fishing line, and eyed the biggest of the three fish below.

What her diorama lacked, Mari thought, deflated, was the attention-grabbing smoothness and glow that the store-bought materials gave. Anyone could tell that little money had been spent on hers. She was glad the projects would be displayed in the library. She wouldn't like to have her diorama in the classroom all day, pointed at when people asked who made the homemade one.

❧

Later, during Natural Science class, Mrs. Graham announced they would go to the library to find out the results of the judging. The students were restless. They talked among themselves in small groups about the hard work they had put into the dioramas. Some admitted how much help they'd had from their parents.

"My dad bought fishing lures and cut the hooks off for me," Jake said behind her. "I'm sure mine's the best!"

Mari couldn't tell which one was best—there were so many beautiful displays. One thing she knew was that her diorama would not get any ribbons. After all, she had not had any help from adults, and it showed.

When they entered the library, Mr. Sims, the assistant principal, and Coach Davis were standing by Mrs. Frank's desk. They were arranging the prize ribbons. Mari guessed they were the judges.

The students gathered around three sides of the large rectangle formed by the tables. The judges stood at one end.

"I'm impressed with the excellent work I see on these tables," Mr. Sims said, smiling and looking from face to face around the room. "Many of the projects show much planning and thought. You've made our job of judging your dioramas very difficult, but we're not complaining about that." The students laughed cautiously and shuffled their feet in place. Mr. Sims continued, "Several projects deserve special recognition. They have been awarded green Honorable Mention ribbons, which are now attached to the winning dioramas."

All the students searched around the room with their eyes to locate their dioramas. Some smiled proudly when they found the green satin ribbon pinned to their work. Mari glanced at hers. There was no ribbon on it.

"Three projects distinguished themselves from the others for the close attention to the subject studied in class and for the detail used in presentation." Mrs. Sims nodded to Coach Davis, who picked up a frilly, white ribbon from the desk.

"Third place goes to Pam Morris," Mr. Sims announced.

The blond girl walked up to Coach Davis to receive her award. Her pale, freckled complexion glowed pink as she accepted the ribbon and thanked him.

"Second place goes to Jeff McIntosh," said Mr. Sims.

Jeff's friends elbowed him teasingly as he made his way up to collect his red ribbon. Coach Davis shook the curly-haired boy's hand.

Mari shrugged her shoulders. She would not get any recognition for her diorama. Maybe it was better this way, no one would figure out which one was hers. She could come back for her project after school, when everyone had left.

"The highest honor of all…" Mari half listened as Mr. Sims continued, "is awarded to someone who worked hard to present the food cycle of Biscayne Bay in a most realistic fashion. The project appears to be a miniature version of what goes on in nature. Very few of the materials used in this model are man-made. This project shows that using your own head and your own hands can be more rewarding than asking for help from others."

Please end this agony, Mari thought, I want to go back to the class before I have to identify my diorama to anyone.

Mr. Sims continued, "First Place goes to Mari Espina."

Mari was jolted back to the room as if from a dream. She had heard her name mentioned. Now Mr. Sims was looking straight at her and holding up a large, frilly blue ribbon.

Her classmates gasped. The room broke out in applause. A few hands reached out to her and gently pushed her forward. Mrs. Graham had a big smile. Mrs. Frank's lips curved happily as she winked at Mari.

Mari stepped forward and shook hands with Mr. Sims and Coach Davis.

"Which one's your diorama?" Mari heard someone ask.

"Yeah, I want to see it," others said.

Mari walked up to her project and pinned the big blue ribbon to the side of the cardboard box.

"It's so realistic!" Cathy said.

"Look at the materials she used," said Erica, clearly impressed.

Mrs. Frank brought out her camera. "Stand by your diorama and hold up the ribbon," she told Mari.

"I'm sure your picture will be put on the library bulletin board. Everyone will see it when they come in," Liz said.

"Better than that," said Mrs. Graham. "We'll have the diorama on display for a month, right here in the library."

"Can I take it home tonight and show my mother?" Mari asked. "I promise to bring it back tomorrow."

"Sure, dear. But right now I want to see a big, fat smile!" said Mrs. Frank, looking through the camera lens.

Mari couldn't hide her pride. A satisfied smile broke out across her face.

"Mamá, look! Look what I won!" Mari yelled happily in Spanish. She had been controlling her excitement since she got home and now she ran to the door as her mother entered their apartment. "I won a ribbon for my project!" Mari held the frilly medallion against her chest so that the long, blue ribbons hung down to her waist.

Mamá reached for the satin streamers and stroked them with her fingers. "It's beautiful! Congratulations!" she told her daughter in Spanish, and smiled lovingly.

"Read what it says," said Mari.

In her best English, Mamá read slowly, "First Place."

"They said mine was the best!" Mari said excitedly in Spanish. "You should have seen the other dioramas. They were so beautiful. But they said mine was the best!"

"Well, I'm not surprised, *mi amor*," Mamá said. "You worked so hard on it every night and it turned out perfect."

"Mr. Sims told everyone they could tell I had worked on the project without any help from others." Mari took a breath and watched her mother's reaction. Mamá smiled and nodded. "You know what, Mamá? Mr. Sims was wrong. I did have some help."

"I don't see how, *mi amor*. You worked alone at this table every night," Mamá said, resting her purse on the kitchen table.

"Well, Mamá," Mari said tenderly. "You gave me the best help anyone could get. You told me to figure things out on my own."

Mamá's eyes filled with tears. "I wish I could have helped more."

"But, Mamá, this was the kind of help I needed. I needed to realize I could do it by myself."

"I'm proud of you." Mamá didn't need to tell her that. Mari already knew. Mamá wrapped her arms around Mari. "Let's take a picture of you standing by your project. In your next letter to Papá, you can send it to him and tell him all about your project and your ribbon."

"Yes," said Mari, grinning happily. "I bet he'll be very proud of me, too!"

Multiple Choices

Chari didn't know if she should be proud or scared. When a fourteen-year old is called to Principal Hill's office, it could be to praise one's good work or to make the dreaded phone call to one's parents to tell them of the latest misdeed. Chari had never given the principal cause to call her parents, which was good, since they spoke little English and the principal knew no Spanish at all. Chari always got excellent reports on her conduct. As for her grades, she had plenty of reason for pride. So she wondered, as she rushed down the hall, why she had been called out of History class.

"Where are you going in such a hurry?" her friend, Lindy, called, standing by a bank of lockers.

"The principal wants to see me," Chari said as she rushed toward the office.

"Are you in trouble?" Lindy asked. Her long, blond hair streamed behind her as she hurried to keep pace with Chari.

"I don't know. I haven't done anything I shouldn't."

"I bet someone took down your name when the food fight broke out in the cafeteria yesterday."

Chari's brown eyes opened wide. "I hope not. I didn't have anything to do with that."

Lindy smiled and winked knowingly at her friend. "Sure you did. Your beautiful, honey-colored hair attracts Mike and his friends like buzzing bumble bees! That's why the boys joined us at lunch."

"I didn't ask him or his friends to sit with us." Chari shrugged, but she felt secretly happy to hear that. Mike was really cute. "Besides, the girls left as soon as it started."

"I know. We don't want any part in such childish games." Lindy stopped by the door to her classroom. "Good luck! Let me know what happens."

Chari followed the wide hallway that led to the administration office. Breathing hard, she paused before entering the bright blue double doors. She wasn't sure if she was winded by her fast pace or by the nervousness that now overtook her.

Lindy, Meg, and Lisa were her new friends. Though she'd longed to be part of the popular group of American girls, she had only recently been included. Maybe they recognized her athletic ability, or maybe it was her perfect pronunciation of English that helped her blend in, she wasn't sure. She only hoped they had become friends because of her fun personality.

Chari didn't think any less of her Cuban friends Isabel and Cristi. They had shared and understood all her fears and struggles in a new country. But this new group was fun and so popular with the boys!

The boys had joined the popular girls at lunch the day before. Showing off, they had flicked peas and carrots to other kids at nearby tables. Chari had left the cafeteria right away. She didn't like to be involved in trouble.

She would tell Mrs. Hill the truth. Chari had never been singled out by her teachers for bad behavior. She had never been called into the principal's office for a problem. Mrs. Hill would understand.

Taking a deep breath, Chari opened the blue door on the right. The bright lights and the stark office furniture made Chari feel she was entering an interrogation room. She shuddered.

The office secretary asked her to wait and, moments later, Mrs. Hill appeared at her door.

"Good morning, Chari." Her smile was warm. "Come on in and we'll have a talk."

Chari got up and followed. Her feet felt like lead. This is my last chance to escape, she thought. I can still run away. But she knew better.

Mrs. Hill pulled up a chair for her. "I've been keeping an eye on your work," Mrs. Hill broke the silence.

Chari's hands were laced tightly on her lap. Her knuckles were white.

"Your grades are very good. Your teachers tell me you are one of their best students." Mrs. Hill paused, watching Chari through red-rimmed eyeglasses.

Surely, Mrs. Hill is wondering why such a good student would be involved in the food fight. Chari felt a wave of heat rush to the tops of her ears.

"Back in December," Mrs. Hill continued, "the teachers selected students who were outstanding for their grades and behavior. These students were to take part in the Leadership Program. You were one of the nominees. Do you remember?"

"Yes, ma'am," Chari said. Her mouth felt dry. She had been told of the program back then, but had not been asked to do anything for it yet, and it was already February.

"I have a very delicate assignment to put into your hands. This job requires an understanding, patient person, a student who can be sensitive to the needs of another." Mrs. Hill adjusted her glasses so that now they rested higher on her nose. "I have selected you because I know you will do a fine job."

Chari nodded with relief. Her visit to the principal's office was not about the food fight. She wasn't in trouble. She felt more at ease.

"A student has transferred from another school. She's going to need help learning her way around and catching up on her classes. As part of the Leadership Program, I'm asking you to take the role of assistant to her. Show her where her classrooms are; how things work in our school; sit with her at lunch. In short, I want you to be her friend."

"I can do that." Chari gave Mrs. Hill a confident shrug.

"This is a permanent pass," said the principal, handing Chari a red, plastic rectangle with the word *Pass* carved on it. On the back, a paper sticker read: *Chari Lopez, Homeroom 9-12.* "With this, you can be excused by your teachers whenever you need to help her."

Chari smiled. She liked this part of the job.

"The new girl doesn't speak much English. You will have to help her with the language."

"That's fine. You know I speak Spanish, too." Chari's voice sparkled with enthusiasm.

Mrs. Hill shook her head slowly. "Well, Yvette doesn't speak Spanish either. She speaks Creole. She's from Haiti and hasn't lived in Miami too long."

"But, Mrs. Hill, I don't speak Creole. I know it's like French, but I don't speak French either." Chari was suddenly afraid of the difficult job assigned to her.

"You'll figure things out. I have confidence in your ability." Mrs. Hill rose, opened the door and signalled her secretary.

Within moments, a short, black girl appeared. Her dark hair was pulled back into a short ponytail which burst into a puff of tiny ringlets. Her large, round eyes turned up slightly at the corners. The tip of her wide nose pointed up, giving her a youthful appearance, hardly in keeping with ninth grade.

"I want you to meet Yvette Pierre, your new friend," Mrs. Hill said, putting her hands on the Haitian girl's shoulders. Then, speaking slowly to make herself understood, she continued. "Yvette, this is Chari Lopez. Chari will help you learn about our school."

A shy grin slowly crossed Yvette's face.

Chari smiled back. She seemed to be a sweet girl. Yet, Chari wondered how much English the girl understood.

"Although this assignment is only for a few weeks, I hope the two of you will be friends for a long time. Let me know if you need my help." With that, the principal walked the girls to the door of the Administration Office.

❧

Chari and Yvette stepped into the wide hallway. They stared at each other in embarrassed silence. Chari wasn't sure what to do next, or even how to speak to Yvette, for fear she would not understand.

She guessed that Yvette needed to find her classrooms.

"Do you have a list of your teachers?" Chari asked, pronouncing each word carefully and slowly. Looking at the girl's blank expression, she rephrased her question. "A list of your classes?"

"Ah! Yes," Yvette's face lit up. She reached into her brightly colored notebook and took out two pieces of paper. "For you," she said, handing Chari one. "For me." She smiled and looked at the paper she held in her hand.

Chari glanced at the clock on the wall and decided Yvette should be in her first class of the day, Math, room 103.

"Come with me. I will take you to this class," Chari said, and pointed to the correct line on the paper Yvette held.

They walked down the hall in silence. Chari glanced at Yvette a few times and smiled, but she didn't speak. She didn't want to make it difficult for the new girl with useless talk she might not understand. Chari could remember her own struggles when she'd first arrived from Cuba. It had been painful to swim in a sea of strangers and to not understand what was being said.

When they arrived at the door to the classroom, Chari pointed to the numbers above the door. "See? One, zero, three." She took Yvette's finger and traced the same numbers written on her schedule.

"One, zero, three," Yvette said in English, with a deep French-sounding accent.

"Math. Mathematics." Chari searched the girl's face for a sign of understanding.

"Yes. Math." Yvette smiled.

"Show this to your teacher," Chari said, pointing to the schedule.

Yvette nodded her head.

"When the bell rings," Chari said slowly, "wait for me here." She pointed to the spot on the floor where they stood.

"Yes, I wait." Yvette's eyes were wide open. Chari thought she read fear in them. "Thank you, Ch-a-r..."

When she saw Yvette had trouble with her name, Chari took a pencil from the girl's hand. She spelled out her name on Yvette's notebook. "Chari," she pronounced clearly.

"Chari," Yvette repeated.

"You wait for me here, O.K.?"

"O.K."

Chari left her and headed back to her own classroom. Halfway down the hall, she turned and saw that the new girl had not entered her room yet. Perhaps Yvette had misunderstood what Chari had said and was waiting for her now. But a closer look showed her Yvette's black eyes were closed and her hands were clasped as if in prayer. Then the girl opened her eyes and reached for the door handle.

When she saw Chari watching her, she waved before entering the room.

❧

After each class, Chari had hurried to Yvette's side and had showed her the way to the next classroom. She now scurried past the mob of students rushing about in the hallways, to meet Yvette for lunch.

"There you are!" Lindy grabbed her elbow and forced her to stop.

"We haven't talked to you all day. You've been in a hurry after every class," said Meg.

"Well, I'm in a hurry now, too," Chari told her friends. "I've got to meet somebody."

Lindy gasped loudly. "The principal?"

Chari shook her head, laughing. "No. I'm not in trouble. Mrs. Hill wants me to help a new student. I'm meeting her for lunch now."

"You're having lunch with the principal?" Meg asked, pretending to be astonished. Meg and Lindy burst out in laughter.

"You two are impossible!" Chari said. Their giggling was contagious and she couldn't help joining them. "I'm having lunch with the new girl."

"Well, come on. We're heading to the cafeteria now." Lindy made room for Chari between herself and Meg. The girls began to leave.

Chari waved them off. "I'll see you there. I have to meet the girl at her class. She doesn't know her way around."

Yvette smiled broadly when she spotted Chari approaching.

"You thought I had forgotten you?" Chari reached her and they worked their way to the lunch room.

"Oh, no. I know you don't forget," Yvette said with a confident smile.

Through short questions during the day, Chari had learned that Yvette knew basic English words, which she pronounced with a nasal French lilt to her voice. Chari liked the sound, even if she had trouble making out what the girl meant sometimes.

When Chari opened the door to the cafeteria, they were hit with the mouth-watering smell of warm food and the loud talk and laughter of hundreds of kids just freed from classes for lunch.

"Are you hungry?" Chari asked.

"Yes. I have my food. I have money for milk." Yvette's black, round eyes questioned her. "You show me how to buy milk?"

"It's easy. You will see. I have to buy some, too." Chari led the way. "Follow me."

They stood at the end of the snaking line of hungry students, each holding a tray and a napkin. The boys ahead of them made loud growling noises, challenging each other for the most obnoxious display. It sounded as though a pack of hungry wolves had been let loose. Chari rolled her eyes at Yvette and shook her head. Yvette gave her a broad smile. Her teeth sparkled as white as fresh coconut.

"You have sisters?" Yvette asked when they sat down to lunch.

"No. I don't have any sisters. I have a younger brother."

"I have two brothers!" Yvette said, happy to discover they had something in common. "They are little. How you say? Youngr…"

"Younger," Chari said, helping her along.

"Brothers no good. They no fun. A sister? That is fun! I have no sister, too."

Chari laughed. She felt the same way. Her little brother was a pest.

From the corner of her eye, Chari saw Mike. She felt a warm sensation rush up the back of her neck. He waved to her as he walked by and sat down with her friends, Lindy, Meg, and Lisa. Chari was sorry she was not a part of their group right now. They seemed to be having fun.

"Chari! Come sit with us!" Meg shouted from across the room.

"Not today." Chari waved to her friends. She knew Yvette needed attention on her first day in this school. It was right that she spend time with her.

"They are your friends?" Yvette asked. "Go to them, if you want."

"Oh, no. That's O.K. I want to spend time with you." Chari was afraid that Yvette would read her true feelings. She really wanted to join her friends' fun, but she stuck by her decision to spend time with the new girl.

❧

For the next few days, Chari joined Yvette for lunch. She no longer needed to walk her to her classes. Yvette could now find her way around.

Chari's friends kept insisting she join the group for lunch. At times she felt she was missing all the fun as she watched them from a distance, but Yvette had not made many friends yet. English was still very hard for her, so Chari sat with her.

Chari helped Yvette with the new language. She remembered the times when she was learning English. It had been difficult and scary, so it felt good to make it easier for someone who was going through the same hard times.

Mrs. Hill had placed a great responsibility in Chari's hands, and Chari wanted to show her that she could do the job. But when Lindy, Meg, and Lisa waved Chari over to their table again, Chari decided to ask Yvette to join them.

"Come with me. I want you to meet my friends." Chari lifted her tray of food from the table.

Yvette's eyes opened wide. "You think they understand my words in English?"

"Sure. You're learning fast," Chari said, expecting her to follow. "I think it's time you practiced with others. You'll make new friends that way."

"Here she comes!" Lindy shouted. "She's finally joining us!"

The girls made room for Chari and Yvette to sit.

"Who's your friend?" Lisa asked, shaking her milk carton before she opened it.

"This is Yvette," Chari answered, as she pulled out a chair. "Yvette, meet my friends Lindy, Meg, and Lisa."

"Hi, Yvette," they all said as one.

Yvette smiled shyly at Chari's friends.

"Yvette is learning English. She's new to the school." Chari opened her milk carton and slipped in a straw.

"Where are you from?" Lindy leaned forward to look at Yvette.

"I come from Haiti," Yvette pronounced each word carefully.

Lisa offered Yvette some corn chips from the open bag. "How do you like our school?" she asked.

Yvette looked puzzled. After a moment, she reached into the offered bag. "Yes, I like these. Thank you."

The girls were quiet with embarrassment. Yvette had misunderstood the question.

Chari helped her out of this quiet moment. "Lisa wants to know if you like our school," Chari said carefully.

"Ah, yes. I like it," Yvette said with a smile.

"Are you doing all right in your classes?" Meg asked. When Yvette looked from Meg to Chari for help, Meg worded it differently. "Can you understand your teachers?"

"I understand, sometimes," Yvette finally said.

"Chari, we're having softball practice after school tomorrow," Lindy reminded her, taking a bite of her sandwich.

"Do we have enough people for a team now?" Chari asked.

"Yes. We even have a few girls waiting for a chance to be on our team," Lindy said with her mouth full.

"We're playing great!" Lisa assured everyone.

"We're going to be the best!" Meg jumped up with excitement.

"What is a team?" Yvette asked Chari quietly while the other girls talked.

"It's a group of girls who play softball together," Chari explained.

A bag of potato chips was passed around. The girls each took one, then waited to bite at the same time, the chips breaking in their mouths with a loud crunch. The girls exploded with laughter at their musical ability.

Yvette stared at the group. She smiled, unsure what the laughter was all about.

Turning to Yvette, Meg said, "You should come to the field and watch us sometime."

Yvette nodded her head. Yet there was no sign of understanding in her black eyes.

"Oh, Chari! The group is planning a beach party," Lindy said, suddenly remembering.

"That sounds great! I can't wait to get some sun," Chari said, her voice rising with joy.

"Mike and his friends are coming, too." Meg dragged out the words slowly. Lisa and Meg winked at Chari, who felt the heat rise to her cheeks.

Chari shrugged. She liked Mike, but she wasn't going to let anyone know how she felt. They would tease her forever.

❧

"I want you to come to my birthday party," Yvette announced as she and Chari walked back to class.

"You're having a birthday? How old will you be?"

"I will be fifteen-years old." Yvette held up her head proudly.

"Oh. I just turned fourteen," Chari said, looking closely at Yvette who was small in comparison.

"You are so much bigger," Yvette said with surprise. "When I started school in this country, *Manman* said it is better if I stay in the same grade. She says it will be easy to learn English this way."

"I know. Some of my Cuban friends repeated a year for the same reason. I guess I didn't have to. I learned English very fast."

"*Manman* wants to meet you. I told her all about you. She knows what a great girl you are."

Chari shoved her gently. "You shouldn't have told her that! I'm not that good!" She laughed.

"She's making a cake for my birthday. Will you come?"

"Sure. Just let me know when it is and I'll be there."

"My party is Sunday, at two o'clock." Yvette smiled proudly. "I'm glad you're coming. I want my family to meet you."

❧

After school, Chari and Lindy went to the mall. Chari wanted to buy Yvette's birthday present. She asked Lindy what she thought of a bright blue T-shirt with a summery design on the front.

"I love it. I'm sure Yvette will like it, too," Lindy said, rubbing the cotton fabric between her fingers. "If she doesn't like it you can buy it for me!"

"Oh, yeah? Right! Your birthday is not for another six months!" Chari watched, amused, as her friend laughed at her own joke.

"I can always come up with a good reason to get presents." With a finger, she pointed to her head, pretending to concentrate. "How about: 'National Best Friends Day?' It's coming up soon, you know."

Chari burst out in laughter. "Oh, hush! There's no such thing!" Chari shook the shirt in front of Lindy's face. "Come on. You're supposed to help me decide."

"I told you, I like the shirt," Lindy said. She raised her hands as if annoyed to be asked again.

"I do, too. It reminds me of a sunny beach day," said Chari, running her fingers over the design.

"Oh, I'm glad you said that. The beach party is this weekend. Everybody is going. It's going to be great!"

"I can't wait! I've got a new swimsuit that I just love," Chari said happily.

"You'd better wear it, because Mike will be there..." Lindy pinched her friend gently in the ribs. "He told me to be sure you go."

"You're kidding! He said that?" Chari felt her blood pulsing faster.

Lindy laughed at the look of pleasant shock on Chari's face. "My mom's driving us. We'll pick you up Sunday at two."

Suddenly, Chari's pleasure turned to horror. "I can't go."

"What do you mean you can't go? This will be the best beach party ever!" Lindy insisted.

"That's the date of Yvette's birthday party," Chari said with regret.

"Well, just tell her something else came up." Lindy raised her shoulders with disregard, as if she had solved the problem.

"I can't do that. I already told her I'd be there." Chari shook her head.

"So now you're going to leave us for your new friend?" Lindy placed her hands on her hips. "You've hardly spent any time in school with us lately, ever since you started hanging around with her."

"I'm her only friend in school so far. How can I cancel out on her birthday party?" Chari begged for understanding.

"I guess it's a tough one," Lindy said, kicking the leg of the clothes rack. "You've got to come up with something. You can't miss the beach party!"

"I don't know. I'll think about it." Disappointed, Chari walked to the register with the shirt. "Let's just pay for this and go home."

❧

"Chari," Yvette called out, catching up with Chari who stood at her locker after school Thursday. "I walk with you, *non?*"

"I'm not going home now," Chari said, selecting shorts and a T-shirt from the crowded mess of her storage locker. "We're having a softball game."

"Oh." Yvette's smile disappeared. She aimed her eyes down at her notebook nested in her arms.

Chari searched for her glove, but didn't miss the look of disappointment on Yvette's face. Chari knew she should ask Yvette to join them. Maybe she would meet other friends this way. "We're playing in the school field. It's just a practice game with my friends. Do you want to come and watch?"

"Yes, I like that." Yvette's dark eyes had a happy glow to them once more.

Chari put away her books and closed the door to her locker with a loud, metallic bang. They walked through the now empty hallways to the girls' rest room.

"I have to change into messy clothes," Chari told Yvette. "Will you hold my glove for me?"

"Yes, I wait." Yvette smiled. She leaned on the wall to wait for Chari, who had entered a stall. Yvette inspected the large leather glove.

"Do you know how to play softball?" Chari asked through the closed door.

"What is softball?"

"It's like baseball, but the ball is bigger and softer."

"Oh, yes. I play baseball with friends in Haiti. I am good," Yvette said proudly, chuckling.

Maybe she could be a strong player on our team, Chari wondered. Thinking Yvette needed a chance to make new friends, Chari said, "Maybe you can try out for our team. Would you like that?"

"What is 'try out?'" Yvette's round eyes questioned Chari as she stepped out wearing her grubby clothes.

"That's when you show others how well you can play."

"I can do that." Yvette had slipped her hand into the glove and now flapped it open and shut. "I know how to hit the ball. And I run fast, too."

"Great!" said Chari, taking back the leather glove. "We can always use another good player on our team."

Ignoring the boys' teasing calls when she arrived on the field, Chari dropped her school clothes on a bleacher. She ran to Lindy and Meg. "Yvette says she's a good player. Why don't we let her try out?"

"We already have all the players we need," said Meg, hitting the center of her glove with her bare fist.

"Did you tell her you can't go to her birthday party?" Lindy asked in a hushed tone.

"No. I haven't talked to her about it yet," Chari said, unable to look her friend in the eye. "If she's a good player, we could use her on our team," Chari insisted, quickly changing the subject.

"Does she know enough English to follow directions?" Lindy asked, glancing at the girl, who stood by Chari's belongings on the other side of the fence.

"Sure she does. And whatever she doesn't understand, she'll figure out. That's how you learn another language."

"All right, we'll give her a chance to try out." Lindy shrugged her shoulders. "Let her borrow a glove and tell her to go to second base."

Chari ran back to Yvette. "Here's my glove. They want you on second base." She patted Yvette's shoulder. Then looking down, she noticed Yvette was wearing black leather shoes. "I think your shoes are too fancy for this."

"I know. I will play with no shoes." She slipped the leather shoes off and placed them side by side on the bleachers, next to her books. Then, with a grin, she ran to her position.

The first girl at bat got a hit. She ran to first base as the others cheered her on. The ball was thrown back to Lindy who was taking a turn at pitching.

Gripping the chain-link fence with her fingers, Chari watched from behind home plate. Mike and his friends sat on the bleachers and cheered and booed every move by the girls.

The next batter passed up on the first pitch. "Ball!" a boy working as umpire yelled.

Lindy kept an eye on the girl on first base, who held one foot on the bag and leaned forward in preparation to run. The tall, blond girl at bat practiced a swing.

Lindy threw a straight pitch this time. The bat met the ball with a loud, clean sound. The ball flew toward center field, too high for Lindy to catch.

"Go for it!" Yvette's teammates yelled. The crowd hollered, excitedly. Yvette ran for the ball and stretched her arm to reach it. The speeding ball hit the tip of her glove and continued flying past her. Yvette then chased it into the outfield.

Chari clenched her fingers tightly on the fence. She hoped Yvette would turn back and cover her base. She should leave that ball for the outfielders.

The girl who had been on first ran past second base and on to third. The blond batter ran close behind.

"Go back to second!" Yvette's teammates shouted.

Yvette leaned down to pick up the ball and came face-to-face with Meg, who quickly grabbed the ground ball and threw it back to the pitcher.

"You should have stayed by your base!" Meg said to Yvette. "I could have thrown you the ball and she would be out now!" Meg pointed to the batter racing for home.

"Home run! We scored two runs!" the girls on the other team cheered. The boys laughed.

Chari watched from behind the fence as her teammates shook their heads, annoyed. She had hoped Yvette would play well. Chari didn't want her to feel embarrassed in front of everyone. Besides, Chari had spoken for her thinking the girl was a good player. Chari had reason to be embarrassed, too.

Lindy approached Chari and ordered softly, "Go take her place."

"So soon? She hardly had a chance to warm up," Chari said. "Give her another chance."

"We'll give her a turn at batting when we're up. But for now, I want you back on the field." Lindy ran back to the pitcher's mound.

Chari patted Yvette on the back when she reached second base to replace her. Yvette handed back the glove, but her ready smile was gone.

When Yvette's turn came to bat, Chari helped her select a bat that was right for her small size. Then she squeezed Yvette's arm and wished her luck.

The tall blond was at the pitcher's mound. She had the muscular build of an athlete. She rubbed the ball in her glove and prepared to pitch. The ball came fast and straight over home plate. Yvette's arms never moved. The bat didn't swing. Only her curly eyelashes batted up and down in surprise.

"Strike one!" yelled the umpire.

The pitcher waited for Yvette to take a practice swing before she pitched the second ball. This pitch was as clean as the first. Sitting on a bench behind the fence, Chari cringed. Yvette swung the bat with all her might, but it didn't make contact with the ball.

"Strike two!" the umpire said to a hushed crowd.

Chari didn't dare look at her friends for fear she might read disappointment in their eyes. Instead, she crossed her fingers and rolled her eyes skyward. Chari said a silent prayer for Yvette on this last try.

The third pitch came as fast and sure as the other two. Yvette swung the bat a fraction of a second after the ball passed over home plate. The force of her unrestrained swing caused her body to continue swirling, so that she faced the crowd when she came to a stop.

"Strike three!"

Chari closed her eyes and took a deep breath. Oh, brother! Yvette had assured her she was good at baseball.

Chari joined Yvette as she rounded the corner of the fence. "Don't worry. Everybody has bad days," she said to make the girl feel better about her terrible performance.

"I have a *very* bad day today!" Yvette said. She chuckled, but Chari could tell from the way she avoided her eyes that Yvette was hurting. "I will go home now."

"You're going to leave?"

"I don't want everyone to look at me. I see you tomorrow for lunch, *non?*" Yvette wiped the red clay from her feet and slipped on her shoes. Chari noticed that she didn't look up, not even when the crisp sound of a hit by the next batter could be heard.

"Sure, we'll have lunch together tomorrow."

❧

The cafeteria line was loud and long. Chari and Yvette stood at the end of it. Chari didn't mind the wait or the loud distractions. She had to break the news to Yvette that she had not made the softball team. Though she sensed that Yvette had figured it out after her performance, it was still hard to be the one to tell her.

She also planned to tell Yvette she would not go to her birthday party. Chari would say that she had something else to do that day, which she had forgotten about. She had wrapped Yvette's birthday present and held it in a paper bag under her arm. Chari planned to give it to her at lunch to ease Yvette's disappointment.

Chari feared backing out of the party more than telling Yvette about not making the team. Yvette had shown a lack of skill at playing the game, so Chari could bring that up. But skipping the birthday party was different. She felt guilty and uncomfortable as she rehearsed her excuse.

"I ask *Manman* for more money today," Yvette said with a twinkle in her eye.

"You're not getting enough to eat at lunch?" Chari opened her eyes wide and laughed nervously.

"It is not for me." Yvette gave her a teasing grin, holding on to the secret a little longer. "I want to buy one of those giant chocolate-chip cookies. It will be for you."

"Oh, I love those! Thank you, Yvette."

"*Non*, I thank you for inviting me to the game yesterday."

Chari froze. Yvette had brought up one of the subjects she hated to have to discuss. "You don't have to buy me anything for that," Chari said, and waved her hand to dismiss the idea.

"It was nice that you let me—how you say?— 'try out?'"

Chari shrugged her shoulders. "Oh, that was nothing." But it was a big deal. She had been embarrassed by the way Yvette had played. And she still had to tell her she was off the team. It was so hard to give someone bad news.

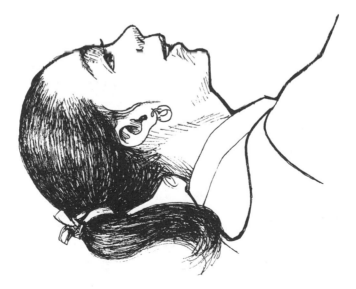

"I had a good time." There was no smile on Yvette's face to back the meaning of her words.

Yvette was making this harder. Maybe Yvette thought she played well enough to be part of the team, Chari wondered with concern. She would have to say something now, even if it hurt Yvette's feelings. Chari took a silent gulp.

"Yvette, I'm afraid you didn't make the team. The girls didn't think you played well enough. I'm sorry."

Yvette's eyes blinked nervously, but she shrugged her shoulders as if the subject wasn't very important. "I know that. I know it yesterday. I play bad!" She chuckled.

"I know you weren't prepared. You didn't have the right clothes or the right shoes. Running barefoot isn't easy."

"Oh, it is not the feet. It is the whole body. It did not work for me." Yvette shook her head, her eyes downcast. "Girls don't play sports in Haiti. Not too much."

"But you said you had played baseball," Chari exclaimed with surprise.

"Yes, I play sometimes. Boys and girls in the neighborhood play in the street, or in a park. But girls don't play in school."

"I know what you mean," Chari said to reassure her. "My family is amazed that I am athletic. Cuban girls don't usually play sports either. Even my Cuban friends in school can't understand."

"I still buy you a cookie! O.K.?" Yvette asked with a warm smile.

"O.K. You can do that." Chari nodded and accepted Yvette's way of saying thanks. The lunch line was moving along. Chari nudged Yvette softly to get her going.

Chari's friends waved as they passed her in the food line.

"We'll see you at the beach!" Meg said.

"The beach party is going to be great!" Lisa pinched her playfully as she walked by.

Chari's face reddened. She glanced at Yvette quickly and hoped she was unaware of the problem Chari was facing. Yvette was busy picking out the largest, most perfect cookie.

Chari watched her friends sit with the boys and regretted not being able to join them. She made her decision right then. She would follow through with her plan.

Chari handed Yvette the package when they sat down for lunch. "I have something for you, too."

Yvette took the paper bag and dug into it with her hand.

Chari cleared her throat. It took all the courage she had to begin talking. "It's your birthday present. You see I'm not going to be able—"

"It's beautiful!" Yvette cut her off. "The paper! The ribbon! You make this package so beautiful yourself?"

"Yes, I wrapped it." Chari felt the blood rush to her face. Yvette was so proud of the wrapping. She didn't even know what was in the package yet.

"It is too beautiful to open!"

"Well, I brought it to school because I—"

"Because you want to make me feel better about the softball team. You are so nice! I tell *Man-man* everyday 'Chari is a sweet girl.'" Yvette held the package tenderly, rocking it in her arms against her chest.

Chari's ears burned with shame. Yvette had misunderstood her selfish act for kindness.

"*Manman* say your name should be *Cherie* and not Chari. It means 'darling' in French, you know. And that's what you are, a 'darling.'"

Chari thought of the true meaning of her name. Chari was just her nickname. In Spanish, she was called *Caridad*, which meant "Charity" in English. She knew she wasn't living up to her name.

"I will take the package home just like it is. I want everyone to see how beautiful you make it." Yvette ran a finger down the bright yellow satin ribbon. "I will open the present with you at the party, *non*?"

Chari nodded her head in shameful defeat. "I will be there."

❧

She wasn't surprised when Lindy called her on the phone to find out if she had talked with Yvette.

"I can't believe you didn't tell her! The party is tomorrow!" Lindy said excitedly.

"It's very hard to tell someone something that isn't true," Chari responded softly.

"You just can't miss the beach party! We're going to play volleyball. Meg's bringing her boombox and her new tapes. One of the boys' dad is grilling hot dogs. I can't wait for the fun!"

"I don't want to miss it. I wish things hadn't worked out this way. I just don't know what to do." Chari rolled the phone cord around her finger nervously.

"Well, today is your last chance to call her and tell her you can't go to her birthday party," Lindy reminded her.

"I know." Chari nodded her head sadly. "Maybe I can tell her I'm too sick to go."

"Sure. They wouldn't want you there, sneezing all over the food and getting all the other guests sick. Yvette will understand."

When Chari was silent for a few moments, Lindy continued. "My mom and I will come by your house tomorrow. I'll see you then."

Chari hung up the phone slowly. She sat on her bed. Drawing her knees up to her chest, she wrapped her arms around them.

It wasn't fair. If she had known the date of the beach party, she could have said no to Yvette when she asked.

She had tried to help Yvette make friends, but it hadn't worked out. Chari couldn't help it if Yvette couldn't do a thing right out in the baseball field. She had stuck her neck out for Yvette and the girl had only embarrassed her with her lack of ability.

I just won't go to the birthday party, Chari thought. They won't miss me with all the friends and relatives that will be there. Besides, she already has my present.

❦

The next day, Chari stared into the mirror as she tried on her new bikini. Somehow, the look wasn't right. She knew she should be dressing for a birthday party instead.

Deep in her heart, Chari knew she would be missed. Yvette was looking forward to Chari celebrating with her. She wanted her family to meet her school friend. And *that* was what Chari had become to Yvette. A friend.

Wasn't that what Mrs. Hill had asked Chari to do? She wanted Chari to be a friend to Yvette. Not just a school helper. A friend.

Chari was not the only one embarrassed on the baseball field. Yvette had suffered even more. The birthday party was a special celebration. If Chari didn't go, Yvette's feelings would be hurt again. Their friendship would never be the same. And she had grown to like the sweet, Haitian girl.

She was sorry that she was going to miss the beach party. She knew it would be fun. But it was only March. There would be many other beach parties. After all, in Miami everyone went to the beach all year round.

❧

The apartment building was quiet. Chari wondered if she had the right address as she knocked on the white door. It was exactly two o'clock. Chari expected to hear voices and laughter coming from the party.

"Chari! How pretty you look!" Yvette said happily when she opened the door. "Come in."

Chari stepped in shyly.

"*Manman*, she's here! *Papa*, come and meet Chari!" Yvette shouted with excitement.

Two boys ran into the small living room and stared at the guest. Chari noticed their resemblance to Yvette. Both had the wide, pointed nose that gave Yvette her air of youth.

"Give her room, boys!" Yvette said, laughing. "This is Jean. He is eleven-years old, and this is my little brother, Claude. He is eight-years old."

"Hi!" Chari said to the two grinning boys.

"Hi!" said Claude, whose cheerful eyes looked just like Yvette's. "I'm glad you're here. Now the party can start, and *Manman* will let me taste that delicious cake."

"You don't have an accent," Chari said to the boy, but glanced questioningly at Yvette.

"The younger people learn English faster, you know that. My brothers waited for you to come so they can sing Happy Birthday and eat."

Chari began to understand that she was the only invited guest. "Nobody else is coming?"

"*Non*. Only you. I start making friends in school now. But I don't know them well to invite them to my birthday party."

A thin, short woman stepped into the small living room. She wore a cheerful, flowered dress and smiled warmly at the guest. Behind her, a man grinned shyly. The woman hung a dish cloth on the back of a dinette chair and motioned for Chari to take a seat on the beige sofa.

"This is *Manman* and *Papa*. This is Chari." Yvette pointed to Chari, then turned to her and said, "*Manman* is just learning English, so I will tell you what she says."

"I understand. I have the same problem with Mami and Papi. I have to help them all the time."

Yvette's mother said some words in Creole, and Chari listened, puzzled.

"*Manman* say you're very pretty," Yvette said.

"*Merci*," Chari thanked her, using one of the few words she knew in French. Everyone laughed.

Yvette's father then spoke in what seemed to be the fastest talk Chari had ever heard. The family laughed happily.

"*Papa* says he hopes you're hungry, 'cause he made the best *griot* and *riz et pois* he ever cooked," said Claude.

"But it wasn't really *Papa* who cooked the food. That's why we laughed. It was *Manman*," Jean explained.

"Sit at the table and I'll show you what the food is," Yvette said, bringing steaming dishes from the kitchen.

Chari inspected the food in the serving dishes. "We eat red kidney beans and rice in Cuba, too. And I love plantains."

"We call them *banane*," said Claude with a big grin.

"*Griot* is fried pork chunks," Yvette said as she dished some onto Chari's plate.

At the end of the meal, Yvette's father brought a round cake with white icing to the table. The fifteen candles glowed. So did Yvette's face.

The Pierre family began to sing the familiar Happy Birthday song in English, with different levels of foreign accent. Chari joined the singing group. Yvette's cheerful, black eyes reflected the sparkle of the candles.

When Yvette opened the present Chari had given her, she proudly passed the blue T-shirt around for everyone to see. Chari held it in her lap for a few moments and stared at the beach scene printed on it. Her other friends were at the beach party now. But Chari had no regrets.

American Girls

Tere slouched in her desk chair, her head lining up behind Mary Beth Jackson's, the blond girl seated in front of her. She didn't want the teacher to see her.

"On what sea does Greece border?" Mrs. Martin repeated. She glanced at the young faces, many of them looking down at their hands.

Mar Mediterraneo, thought Tere in Spanish. She knew the answer. After all, geography was one of her favorite subjects. It was just too difficult to say it in English.

"I want to see more hands up. Let's hear from some students who haven't spoken lately," said Mrs. Martin firmly as she paced in front of the chalkboard.

From the corner of her eye, Tere saw a few other hands going up. She hoped this would satisfy the teacher. Tere wished Mrs. Martin would stop looking for answers from the quiet students. She pulled her shiny, brown hair forward like a dark curtain, hiding her face.

The Miami midday sun was warming the classroom. But the warmth that rose in Tere's body was from fear. She dreaded being called on by the teacher.

Mrs. Martin called on a boy two rows behind Tere. Tere felt more relieved, for now.

Brian was tall, slim, and had sandy brown hair. He didn't raise his hand in class often. Yet, many times he laughed and cut up with his friends across the room.

The boy glanced at his friends with a smug smile. "The *Medickrrenean* Sea," Brian said with trouble.

Snickers could be heard around the room.

"That's good. You've got the idea. The name is *Med-i-ter-ra-nean.*" Mrs. Martin pronounced the word slowly.

"Who can tell me what's the capital of Greece?" Mrs. Martin continued. Tere felt the fear again. Many hands went up, waving in the air.

Tere sank further in her seat. If the teacher kept asking questions, chances were Tere's turn would come up. She sat still, her eyes fixed on her clammy hands.

"Name the capital of Greece," Mrs. Martin said again to the class.

"*Atena*, of course," Tere said silently to herself.

Mrs. Martin left her place by the chalkboard in the front of the room and walked between the rows of desks. Tere feared she couldn't hide anymore.

The English-speaking students had it so easy. All they had to do was study and they had the answer. She had to translate some of the words into Spanish, her first language, so she could understand what she read. Yet, the worst part was learning to pronounce the English words. Every time she said something in public, it just didn't sound right. She had seen the smiles on the faces of the other students. She had seen them laugh at her attempts.

Through her dark, lowered eyelashes, Tere followed Mrs. Martin's movements. She stopped two rows over and turned, facing Tere. Tere's brown eyes opened wildly. Her cheeks grew warm when she realized Mrs. Martin's gaze was on her.

"What is the capital of Greece? Tere?" Mrs. Martin's gentle smile did not ease Tere's discomfort.

She had to face the moment. She did know the answer, but could only remember the name in Spanish.

"Mrs. Martin," she said timidly, "I don't know how you say it in English." The class grew quiet, interested in this turn of events. The students in front of her had turned so they could watch the drama. Time was running so slowly for Tere.

"Well, Tere, if you know the answer in Spanish, why don't you give it a try?"

Tere looked down at her cold, wet palms. "The capital of Greece is *Atena*."

The children exploded with laughter. Tere's face burned, the warmth rising to her scalp until she could feel each hair stand at attention. Her head felt tight, like a filled balloon.

"Stop the laughter. Now!" Mrs. Martin shouted in her serious business tone. The class quieted slowly. A few giggles escaped here and there.

Then, she turned back to Tere. "That's correct, Tere. In Spanish it's *A-te-na*?" Mrs. Martin asked, trying out her pronunciation. "The name is Athens in English."

Tere nodded her head. She couldn't say the *th* sound. It wasn't used in her native country, Cuba. She hoped Mrs. Martin would go on to other questions and other students, removing the attention from her.

Mrs. Martin asked the next question. Tere heard her from afar, but she was not listening to the words. She knew she wouldn't be called to answer again soon. She still smarted from the hurtful laughter.

Tere looked across the room at her friend, Alicia. She was Cuban like Tere, but she could speak English well and hardly had a Spanish accent.

A tender, understanding smile was on Alicia's face. Tere knew she could count on her friend. She was sure Alicia had run into this sort of problem before.

❧

The students left the classroom carrying their paper bag lunches. Tere slowed down so that Alicia could catch up with her. As the small group of boys (led by Brian, of course) passed Tere, each of them had a wise remark to make.

"Hello, Atena."

"Walk faster, Atena."

"Hey, Atena. What's for lunch?"

They walked by Tere, doubling over with laughter. Some of the girls joined in the fun, repeating the city's name in Spanish. It seemed Tere had earned a new name.

Tere was hurt and angry, but she ignored their words. Finally, Alicia joined her.

"Don't pay attention to them. They think they're so funny. They just don't know much." Alicia spoke to her in Spanish.

"I try not to listen, but it hurts when they make fun of me." Tere answered her in Spanish, the language she felt most comfortable speaking.

"Just remember that we are way ahead of them. We can speak two languages. They only speak English." She tried to make Tere feel better.

"I guess so." Tere didn't care for the advantage. Right now she wished she was like the others.

"And when they go on teasing, you and I can turn to Spanish. Then, they have no idea what we are saying. It's like our secret code." Alicia winked a pretty brown eye at her friend.

In the cafeteria, Mari was saving seats for them at her table. Mari was in Mrs. Robinson's homeroom, but was able to meet with her friends for lunch.

"The boys were so mean to Tere," Alicia said as she set down her food tray. She told Mari what had happened in class.

"It's bad enough to be called on by the teacher. But, when you are not sure of the answer, it's very hard." Mari agreed with the others.

"But, I was sure of the answer. I studied all this in Spanish before," Tere explained. "It's not as if I'm dumb."

"I know. Sometimes they think that if you don't speak their language you must be slow in the head." Mari's parents were from Cuba, but she had been born in Miami. Mari could speak both English and Spanish well and had no trouble with an accent. She wasn't picked on by the others.

"The school carnival is coming up soon." Alicia changed to a more cheerful subject. "I want to volunteer for a fun booth."

"Me, too. Let's sign up for the same booth," said Mari as she unwrapped her cream cheese and guava jelly sandwich.

"I'll do it if we can all work together." Tere eyed her friend's lunch with delight. "You've got my favorite kind of sandwich! I'll trade you half of my chicken salad on whole wheat for half of yours," she offered Mari.

"Which booth do you think will be the most fun?" Alicia asked.

"I like the Ring Toss. You just collect their tickets and hand them the rings. It's not much work," said Mari, handing Tere her sliced sandwich.

"Yeah, that one or the Bake Sale booth. That way we can choose the best cookies for us to buy," said Tere cheerfully. "We might even get to keep the baked goodies that crumble apart."

This idea brought giggles from the girls. They went on with their Spanish chatter.

"The best cupcakes and brownies tend to crumble, you know..." Tere smiled playfully and winked at her friends.

"Ooh, I like that idea!" Alicia said as she licked her lips. The others laughed.

"Whatever we do, let's make sure we don't get the Pie-in-the-Face booth. That would be more than I can take!" Mari begged.

"Or the Dunk Tank. I don't know which would be more embarrassing," Tere said, shaking her head. Her long, straight hair glittered with the movement.

"I know. Those are for people like Mary Beth Jackson who is so daring," Alicia agreed.

"And so mean," Mari added.

"I bet the boys like those two booths best," Tere guessed.

"Yeah. To work at them and to play. Especially Brian, Karl, Joe and the others. They like messy games that make people look silly," said Alicia.

"Thanks for trading half your lunch." Tere licked her finger where the cheese and jelly had rubbed off.

"You are so funny!" Mari laughed. "Here. Do you want to lick my finger, too?"

"Yuck! All I see on it is celery and mayonnaise." The three girls laughed.

"So, which booth do we choose?" Alicia asked her friends.

"Let's make it the Bake Sale booth," said Mari.

"Great. The three of us will work the 10 o'clock time slot. Don't forget to sign up," Alicia said, finishing the plan.

❧

Tere fretted again, this time in math class. She understood the subject well. She even liked fractions. She could picture in her mind parts of a whole and fit them together as a complete puzzle. Sounding out her answers to the class was the problem. Even if she was often correct.

They had been reviewing homework in Mrs. Baxter's class. Thirty problems had been assigned, just as many as there were students in the class. Mrs. Baxter liked class participation. She liked to call on each student for an answer, and sometimes had a student work out the problem on the board.

Now she called out names in her high-pitched voice. "Jennifer, give us the answer to the next problem."

The curly-haired girl answered, "Two-fifths."

"Thank you, Jennifer." Mrs. Baxter went on calling students without any particular order.

That added to Tere's fear. She couldn't guess which problem would be hers. Tere wanted to mentally practice sounding out her answer.

"Next, problem. Jeremy?" Mrs. Baxter looked from the book to the boy.

He had a head for numbers. Jeremy always had the right answer. And he was nice. You couldn't help but admire someone like him.

"Three-eighths," answered Jeremy.

"Good." Mrs. Baxter looked around the room.

Tere felt her heart jump as Mrs. Baxter looked in her direction. But, fortunately, Mrs. Baxter went on scanning the faces. Tere stared at her paper and hoped the bell would ring before her turn came up.

"Brian, what's the next answer?"

He was an annoying boy. Always first to laugh at others. So sure of himself and yet, wrong so often, thought Tere.

"Four-twentieths," he said with a self-assured nod.

"What's wrong with that answer? Who can tell me?"

Muffled snickers sounded around the room.

A few hands went up. Mrs. Baxter called on Mary Beth Jackson.

The well-muscled girl raised her eyebrows in Brian's direction and smiled confidently. "He didn't take it down to it's lowest common denominator."

"That's right, Mary Beth."

The girl smiled, sweet as an angel, at Brian. He smirked back.

Tere heard her name called out by Mrs. Baxter. She felt hot goose pimples crawl up the back of her neck.

"Oh, no," she thought, "this answer has lots of difficult sounds. I'm doomed."

"Atena..." Tere heard the mean whisper coming from behind. She felt so alone. Her hands shook, making her math paper vibrate.

Mrs. Baxter waited patiently. Tere swallowed hard and spoke.

"*Tree-hundrets.*"

She could hear the laughter. The students' hands were pressed tightly to their mouths, but the sounds still escaped. Mrs. Baxter looked sternly in the direction of the muffled sounds. The noise stopped.

"Very good, Tere. You reduced your answer to the lowest denominator. Three-hundredths." Mrs. Baxter gave her one of her rare smiles.

Tere felt so tired, so low. It seemed every time she opened her mouth in class, the sounds came out wrong. Most people found it funny. Brian and the boys led in the laughter. But the girls also joined in, with Mary Beth Jackson's rolling laugh setting off the others.

Tere's attention wandered. She stared out the window where loud blue jays chased a sparrow off the tree. The little bird flew away and found safety in a tiny hole under the eaves of a school building. Tere understood the sparrow's problem, but she envied him. At least he had a place to hide.

The classroom seemed darker to her. It was so hard to speak up in class, Tere thought. Instead of feeling good about having the right answers, she felt more and more self-conscious about her English. She was studying and could keep up with the work. But now she was beginning to feel it was not worth it. The cost of giving the teachers her answers was too dear.

❧

Tere and Alicia ran to the edge of the school field. Miss Sawyer had sent two other girls to relieve them when their fifteen minutes of soccer practice were up. Now, under the shade of a large oak, they drank water and escaped from the hot Florida sun.

"Look at your neck! You're sweating so much!" Alicia pointed to her friend's collar with a big grin on her face.

Other small groups of girls sat in the shade carrying on conversations of their own. Tere and Alicia spoke in Spanish, as they usually did when they were by themselves.

"Look at you. Your legs are so muddy those socks will never be school colors again." Tere laughed, leaning back on the shady bench.

Alicia examined her regulation socks, normally white with a blue band, but now almost all brown. She shrugged her shoulders.

"Speak English!" The loud voice was Mary Beth Jackson's, who was sitting under the tree with friends. "You are in an English-speaking country!" Her friends laughed, hiding their grins behind their hands.

"A country that can speak? How clever!" Alicia yelled back at the group in English.

"Ignore her," said Tere in Spanish. "She will say anything for a laugh."

"They probably think we were talking about them," Alicia guessed in her native language.

"Let them think what they want. We weren't doing anything wrong or mean." Tere shrugged her shoulders.

"You're gonna have to wash your hair. Your face is red and your hair is clinging to it, all wet," Alicia told her.

"Thanks, you look great yourself!" Tere laughed at her friend's looks, but then grew serious. "Don't you hate it when you have to shower in the locker room? There's not much privacy there."

"Yeah, Miss Sawyer doesn't let you get away with anything. She's always checking towels to make sure they're damp."

"It seems the other girls don't care about undressing in that big room." The school that Tere had attended before had physical education as the last class of the day. The girls then went home to shower in privacy.

"I think it bothers them, too. Haven't you noticed how they run inside, before the teacher makes it in? Even Mary Beth races in," Alicia pointed out. "They rinse their feet in the shower and sprinkle drops of water on themselves with their fingers. When Miss Sawyer walks in, they're drying off, pretending they took a full shower."

Tere smiled. "I guess I'm going to have to learn a few tricks to make it around here," she admitted to her friend.

"I don't think you're going to get away with that today. You're too muddy and wet," said Alicia.

"I know," said Tere. She realized she couldn't put on her clothes, as messy as she was, and go on to the rest of her classes.

"Don't worry, no one looks at anyone else. It's an unwritten law. We all know we have to walk around in there with half our clothes off."

Tere dashed into the locker room as soon as Miss Sawyer blew the whistle marking the end of class. Tere beat Alicia and many others in her rush to the showers. But she removed the sweaty clothes in the curtained stall and took a complete shower. The fresh water ran down her hair and cooled her off.

Suddenly, Tere's white towel was plucked from its hook. A hand had reached over the wall and disappeared with it, before Tere could grab it back. She could hear laughter coming from the next shower stall.

She held her sweaty T-shirt in front of her dripping body. "Alicia! Alicia!" Tere called out for her friend through the closed curtain.

"Where are you?" Alicia yelled back.

"I'm in here, in the shower," Tere called out in Spanish. "Bring me a towel. Quick!"

"Speak English, girls," a voice called out. Although its owner disguised it, Tere knew it was Mary Beth Jackson.

"Did you forget your towel?" Alicia asked Tere in English.

"Did she forget her towel?" Mary Beth Jackson asked, pretending innocence. Her laughter was loud.

"Here's a towel!" Kelly giggled and threw a damp towel over the wall.

"She can use mine!" yelled out Dara through her laughter.

Alicia brought a dry, clean towel to Tere. She turned back to Spanish. "Just get dressed and let's get out of here."

Quickly, Tere dried her skin and put on her underwear. She worked fast. She didn't want to be around the pranksters much longer. She might yell at them and start an ugly fight. Tere took her dry clothes from her locker. She held the towel up with her chin and expertly slipped into her shirt.

"Don't forget, we volunteer for carnival jobs today." Tere said as Alicia joined her, half-dressed and damp. The subject helped them ignore the silly girls who were still delighted by their joke.

Fitting In

"Oh, I won't forget," said Alicia. "We have to raise our hands first so they'll pick us. It's the only way we'll end up together."

"I hope you, me, and Mari end up working the Bake Sale booth. It'd be so much fun to work together."

The girls brushed their damp hair and left the locker room for their next class.

❧

"Please close your books. We're going to take a few minutes to find carnival volunteers," Mr. Taber said, during the last class of the day.

Mr. Taber taught English. He expected the students to practice their speaking skills often. He would ask them to read aloud from a book or from their written work. Mr. Taber wanted his students "to break out of themselves."

This was not Tere's favorite class.

"As I call the name of each carnival booth, I would like to see the hands of those who want to work there."

The students nodded their heads. Tere glanced at Alicia and the two smiled.

"I can only take three volunteers for each booth. It's the only fair way to do it. All other classes will be sending their lists of three volunteers per booth."

Tere thought their chances to be together were good. Mari was in another class, so she would not add to Mr. Taber's list of volunteers.

Mr. Taber explained the rest of his rules: "When you raise your hand, be prepared to tell me what talents you have that would be helpful in this job. I want you to break out of yourselves."

Break out of yourselves, Tere mimicked silently. Oh, brother! Leave it to Mr. Taber to make a fun thing so painful.

She couldn't possibly explain herself in front of the whole class. Not in English. Tere could think of many reasons why she would be good for the Bake Sale booth. But how could she tell Mr. Taber in front of everyone.

"I want volunteers for the Fortune Telling booth," said Mr. Taber.

Four hands went up, all girls. He called on the first three.

"I can come up with good ideas in the blink of an eye. I could tell the people this is what I see as their future," said Dara.

Mr. Taber wrote her name down and called on the next volunteer.

"I have an old fish bowl that I use as a crystal ball and I pretend to tell my friends' fortunes. I have a lot of practice at it," said Jennifer.

Down went her name on the list.

"My family believes I can see the future," said Megan. All the students' eyes were on her now. "I told my sister I had a premonition she would get hurt. Then she had a bad accident on her bike."

"Oh!..." students murmured.

Mr. Taber wrote her name on the list. He went on to name another booth and many hands went up. He called on the first three students to explain their talents.

Tere could see that Mr. Taber didn't question their answers. He simply wanted the students to speak in public.

She rehearsed her answer in her mind. I like to bake and I know math well. No. She couldn't say math. That was a *th* word. I like to bake and I'm good with numbers. There, that's what she would say. But it would still be so hard.

"Next, I want volunteers for the Bake Sale booth," Mr. Taber said.

Two hands went up. Alicia and Andrea had volunteered.

Tere was so afraid to speak up. Her hand trembled as she thought of raising it. Her skin was clammy. She shivered.

Alicia gave her a questioning look from across the room.

"Two volunteers. Very well. Go ahead, Alicia."

Tere had missed her chance. She was already sorry for not raising her hand. Mr. Taber only had two volunteers for this booth. Maybe he would ask for a third one, she silently hoped.

"I like baking and I hope to work in a store," said Alicia.

Now it was Andrea's turn. "My mom is baking lots of cupcakes for the carnival, and I'm working on a sign for the booth."

Surely, Mr. Taber would call for one more person from their class. I like to bake and I'm good with numbers, Tere practiced.

Alicia gave her a funny look. Tere thought she was mad at her for not raising her hand, so she found the strength. She now knew she would speak up. Working in that booth was important to her.

She practiced in her head again, I like to bake and I'm good with numbers.

Mr. Taber started to speak again. Tere was sure he would call for the third Bake Sale volunteer. She quickly raised her hand.

"...volunteers for the Pie-in-the-Face booth," Mr. Taber finished saying.

Tere's mouth opened in horror. She brought her hand down. But it was too late. Mr. Taber was calling her name.

"Tere, Mary Beth and Karl," Mr. Taber said. "Tere give us your reason for wanting this booth."

"But I don't want *dis* job, Mr. Taber." Tere felt an ache in her throat. She hoped she wouldn't cry.

"Your hand was the first one up." Mr. Taber shrugged his shoulders, not understanding her problem. "Now, tell us your talent."

"I *dought* you wanted one more person for Bake Sale," Tere said sadly.

"We were finished with that booth. We had moved on to the next one."

"But, Mr. Taber, I like to bake..." she started to explain, but he stopped her.

"It's not that kind of pie, sweetie," said Mr. Taber, not giving in.

"It's shaving-cream pies!" Brian shouted from across the room. He had raised his hand, but hadn't been fast enough to be selected.

"That's enough, Brian," said Mr. Taber, turning to face him. "Mary Beth, tell us about your talent."

"I like to make people laugh. Messy stuff is my business." She looked around the room happily as the class roared with laughter.

Tere heard the voices in a fog. Messy stuff was the trouble she got herself into because she had been so shy, so afraid to speak and be laughed at. Now she would really be laughed at. She would be the target for the pies!

"I think it's really funny to get a pie in the face. I can laugh it off," Karl was saying with a big grin on his face. The boys were laughing with him.

Tere didn't think it would be funny at all to get a pie in her face. And she wouldn't be with her friends.

Alicia wouldn't look up from her desk. Tere didn't know if Alicia was mad at her or if she just felt sorry for her.

❦

"Mom, please. I don't want to go to school today," Tere begged her mother in Spanish, their home language.

"Tere, I'm sorry you've gotten into such a mess. But, you must face your problems." Mom sprayed her dark brown hair in place. She wore a red suit with a silk scarf around her neck that made her face even prettier.

"I can stay home and catch up on my reading. After all, we're not going to do any school work today. We're only having that stupid carnival."

"I can't leave you alone in the house all day." Mom looked at her sweetly. "Darling, I know that the boys can be cruel, but when you work a booth like that, it's all in fun. Don't let them laugh at you. You laugh with them instead."

"Oh, Mom. You make it sound so easy."

Tere signed up for the ten o'clock time. Alicia and Mari would be working in the Bake Sale booth at the same hour and wouldn't have to see her messy and unhappy.

The back of the booth had a wooden wall with a clown's hair and hat painted on it. The space for the clown's face was cut out for a volunteer's head to fit through. The children exchanged four tickets for a tin plate filled with shaving cream and tried to hit the volunteer's face.

"Look! The Spanish girl is working with us!" Mary Beth Jackson yelled as Tere came into the booth.

"I'm not Spanish. I'm Cuban," said Tere, getting busy with the tin plates.

"OK. So, the Cuban girl is working here."

Tere just shook her head. She started to fill up the plates with the white cream.

"Who's gonna be first at the clown's head?" Kelly was also working the booth. She did everything Mary Beth Jackson asked. Tere was sure Mary Beth Jackson had asked Kelly to work with her.

"I want to be first," said Mary Beth Jackson.

"I'll go next. This is going to be fun!" said Kelly.

"I don't really want to do *dat* job," said Tere to the girls. "I prefer to take tickets and have *de* plates ready."

"That sounds great to me!" Mary Beth Jackson said, running behind the wall. "The fun part is getting hit with the pies."

Soon they had their first customers. Four boys stopped at the counter laughing at the girl's head sticking out of the wall.

"Pay the Cuban girl, and you get to hit me with a pie!" Mary Beth Jackson yelled at them.

Kelly and Tere took their tickets and handed pies to the boys.

"Bet none of you can hit me!" Mary Beth Jackson challenged, and laughed.

A small crowd of children soon gathered to watch the fun.

The first boy tried his hand. His pie hit the clown's hat and slid down the wall.

"Not good enough!" Mary Beth Jackson yelled. "Try again."

The boy's friend threw his pie and also missed. Small droplets of cream landed on the girl's forehead and nose. Mary Beth Jackson laughed.

"You still missed me," she yelled out.

The next pie hit her ear. She screamed with delight.

"You boys stink! Your aim is terrible!"

The crowd had gathered closer and was now clapping and cheering the boys. Tere watched the action, amused. She was glad she didn't have to be the target.

A foamy pie came flying at the clown's face and hit Mary Beth Jackson on the left cheek. The side of her face was covered with the white stuff. She didn't wipe it off.

The crowd loved it. They cheered and yelled loudly. Tere stood in the corner, filling more tins and laughing quietly.

"All right!" Mary Beth Jackson yelled out with laughter. "That's more like it!"

"Come and get it!" Kelly called out to the crowd. "Just four tickets for the chance to hit Mary Beth with a pie!"

"Who's next?" Mary Beth Jackson yelled.

"I want a pie," said Brian as he and his friends moved forward through the crowd.

"Pies for us, too," said Karl. He and Joe waved their tickets in the air.

Tere took the tickets from the boys and handed shaving cream pies to them.

"Look who's working here, guys!" Joe called to others as he took his tin plate.

"Atena! You look nice and clean. When's your turn at the wall?" Bryan asked with a devilish smile on his face.

Tere didn't answer him. She knew it would only cause more teasing.

"OK. Let's see if you guys are any good!" Mary Beth Jackson was ready for more.

The crowd was growing. The children were shouting and cheering. Many wanted a turn. The girls took in more tickets and handed out pies.

Karl hurtled his creamy tin plate and hit Mary Beth Jackson in the center of the face. Everyone laughed excitedly.

"Bull's eye!" shouted Karl proudly.

Mary Beth Jackson blew the shaving cream off her mouth with a loud puff. She poked her hands through the hole to wipe the cream from her eyes.

"Hand me some paper towels," she asked her helpers. "I can't see a thing."

Tere ripped off some of the paper from the roll. She stepped up to the wall to hand it to the blinded target.

"Hey, Atena! Give us a smile!"

Tere didn't have a chance to duck. The foamy pie came flying from the crowd and landed on Tere's face.

Suddenly, the booth was under attack. The filled tin plates came flying across the counter, hitting Tere and Kelly all over their bodies. When the girls turned for protection, they were hit on the back. Kelly's hair had changed from black to white in seconds.

Kelly screamed and laughed. "Stop it! Only one at a time!"

Mary Beth Jackson was missing the action. Her eyes were still covered with cream. "You're supposed to throw the pies at me! I'm the target!" she shouted angrily.

The crowd was wild. They ran out of prepared pies and reached for the cans of shaving cream. They squirted Tere and Kelly as the girls hopped around, trapped within the booth. Then they aimed the squirting nozzles on each other and ran around in a crazy sort of dance.

Tere escaped from the booth and ran to the locker room when she had the chance. Globs of cream fell off her body, leaving a trail of white puffy mounds. She wiped her face with the paper towels she still held in her hand.

In the deserted locker room, Tere looked in the mirror. Her brown hair was clumped with the white stuff. It felt gummy to the touch. Her face was smeared with white streaks so that her pretty brown eyes were all that was recognizable about her.

She saw a smile break out on her whitish lips. She didn't like the cruel teasing, but she had to admit that the messy part was fun.

❧

The next day, Tere and Mary Beth Jackson were called out of Mrs. Martin's class. They were asked to report to the principal's office. Tere knew this would be a difficult visit for her. She had nothing to fear; she knew she had done nothing wrong. But she would be asked about the events at the booth, and she had enough trouble with those boys without becoming a tattletale.

Mrs. Ferro, the principal, wore a gray suit. She always wore a suit, even to outdoor assemblies. It seemed to Tere that she was trying to look serious and intimidating.

Kelly already sat in one of the three chairs facing Mrs. Ferro's desk. She stared wide-eyed at the two girls as they came in.

Some of the loudest boys had been rounded up during the shaving-cream fight, Mrs. Ferro explained. Mr. Taber had been supervising the area and broke up the rowdiness. But he hadn't been there when it started. He hadn't seen the wild behavior building up, so the teachers didn't know which children had started the problem.

"I hear that the three of you were working at the Pie-in-the-Face booth when the trouble began." Mrs. Ferro sat behind her desk. She looked at the girls through her big, round glasses.

Tere nodded her head and saw that the other two did the same.

"What were each of you doing at the time?"

The girls looked at each other uneasily. Mary Beth Jackson spoke up first.

"I was at the clown's face. I was the target getting the pies thrown at me."

"And you, Kelly? What were you doing?"

"I was taking tickets and handing out pies to the kids."

"Tere? What was your job?"

"I was filling *de* pies and taking tickets from *de* kids, too."

"So, all of you saw how it began. You saw who started it."

Tere's mouth felt dry. She gulped dry air.

"I couldn't see a thing," Mary Beth Jackson rushed to explain. "I was hit by a pie smack in the face. My eyes were covered with shaving cream."

"What about you? What did you girls see?"

"I had my back to the crowd when it started. It all went so fast..." Kelly answered quickly. "I had the stuff all over my eyes. I couldn't see either."

Mrs. Ferro looked at Tere and waited for her answer.

"I was busy. I was giving Mary *Besf* some paper towel so she could wipe her eyes."

"But you didn't. You never gave me the paper towels and I couldn't see anything. I had to wipe the stuff away with my fingers. It got in my eyes and it hurt," Mary Beth Jackson said angrily. "When I opened my eyes, you were gone."

"*Dey* hit me *wis de* pies as I walked over to you. *Dere* was a lot going on," said Tere. She saw Kelly nodding her head. "I ran to *de* locker room to get cleaned up as soon as I could."

Mary Beth Jackson yelled at her. "You were supposed to be my helper! You chickened out. You abandoned us." Her eyebrows were knitted together in a fierce look.

"I did not!" Tere defended herself.

"Enough! Girls! That's enough yelling at each other!"

Tere and Mary Beth Jackson quieted down. But Tere could see from the corner of her eye that Mary Beth Jackson was breathing strong angry puffs and was giving her a devilish side-glance.

"Surely you girls heard the voices of the leaders. You would recognize who they were."

The three girls were silent. Tere stared at her hands on her lap while Mrs. Ferro waited patiently for some response. No one spoke up. Finally, the principal sent them back to class.

As they stood up to leave, Mrs. Ferro asked Tere to remain behind. Tere sat back down. Mary Beth Jackson squinted a silent threat in Tere's direction. Tere slouched, defeated, in her chair.

"Who threw the first pie?" Mrs. Ferro asked her as soon as they were alone.

The hair on the back of Tere's neck rose up, as if a lizard had climbed a ladder up to her head.

"Mrs. Ferro, I didn't see it coming. I was facing Mary *Besf wis de* paper towels in my hand."

"Now, Tere. Your behavior in school has always been excellent. Your teachers all report on your good manners and honesty. That is why I have asked you to stay behind." Mrs. Ferro leaned back in her chair. "I'm sure you heard the boys at the counter. You had just handed them pies to throw at the clown. I am hoping you can tell me the names of those who started the fight."

Tere was surprised by a feeling in her chest that seemed to choke her. Her heart beat harder and louder.

Sure, she knew it was Brian and Karl and Joe. They had started it with their mean ways and loud mouths. But Tere couldn't tell on them. Their meanness toward her would grow. She had it tough enough already. Besides, the crowd had been fired up and joined in the foam fight instantly. It seemed to her that everyone was ready for the fight.

"I really didn't see who did it. I don't know many of *de* boys by name. I don't know many of *de* boys at all," Tere told Mrs. Ferro.

Everyone in school knew about it. Brian, Karl, Joe and two others were given detention. They had to come to school on Saturday to rake leaves and clean up any messy areas.

The boys didn't like it. Tere could tell from the way they had carried on. The troublemakers had been quiet in class, and they had clustered in the lunchroom and hallways, whispering.

Alicia, Mari and Tere walked to the main door after school. There, the girls went separate ways every day. Alicia and Mari lived north of the school and walked home together. Tere lived in the opposite direction and walked through the school field alone.

"I think the punishment was too hard," said Alicia. The friends talked in Spanish.

"They got what they deserved," said Mari, stopping to look at Alicia. "They took over the booth and made a mess. No one else had a chance to play that game."

"Yes, I guess they ruined the fun for others," Alicia agreed.

"But the crowd was ready to attack. I think the children would have taken over without Brian leading the pack," Tere assured her friends.

"So, it was Brian who started it?" Mari asked Tere.

"He did. But the others followed right away. They all wanted a messy fight."

"Is that what you told the principal?" Alicia asked in surprise.

"Of course not. I told her I didn't see who started it and that I don't know too many of the boys."

"Well, they think you named all the boys in trouble." Alicia gave her friend a serious look.

"Mary Beth told everyone that the principal asked you to stay behind. She says you must have told, because she and Kelly didn't." Mari looked at Tere, her thick eyebrows raised.

"I didn't tell Mrs. Ferro. Not even when I was alone with her." Tere shook her head. "You know I don't want any more trouble with those boys."

"We didn't think you told on them. But we wanted to warn you," Mari said.

"Yeah, thanks," said Tere, shifting her heavy book bag. "Have a good weekend."

❧

Tere walked to the back gate of the ball field. This was the most direct way home. From there, it was four short blocks of shady sidewalks lined with trees. She often saw school children go this way. Today, there was no one in sight.

Suddenly, she heard hurried footsteps behind the hedge. The bushes shook. She was on guard.

"She's coming! She's coming!"

Tere heard the hushed whispers. She prepared herself for trouble. She wouldn't turn back. It was a long way around. Besides, she would end up on the same street and the boys would still be waiting for her.

Tere decided to be brave and face what they had to say. She had done nothing wrong.

She unlatched the gate and walked out to the other side of the hedge. The group waited. Brian, Karl, Joe and two others were facing her at the small bridge over the ditch. All the boys who had gotten detention were there. So was Mary Beth Jackson.

She took a deep breath and walked toward them.

"Atena, how nice to see you," said Brian with a mocking smile.

"Yes, it's just who we wanted to meet today." Karl grinned at the others.

The boys blocked the entrance to the footbridge and Tere was forced to stop.

"What do you want?" Tere asked them, keeping her head high.

"We want to know what you told the principal, Spanish girl," said Karl.

"We know what she told the principal; we want to know why," shouted Brian menacingly.

"I am Cuban, not Spanish," said Tere proudly.

"What difference does it make, Cuban girl? Just tell us why you told on us." Brian raised his voice angrily.

"I didn't say *anysing* about you, if *dat's* what you mean." Tere tried her best English pronunciation. But the group just laughed anyway.

"You told Mrs. Ferro our names. They called us into her office as soon as you left," shouted Karl.

"Yeah! Everybody knows Kelly and I didn't say anything. You talked to her alone." Mary Beth Jackson joined in the accusations.

"How else would they know our names?" Joe asked.

"You were *dere*. All of you had cans of shaving cream in your hands. *Dat's* how *dey* knew it was you!"

"There were many kids in the fight. But only the five of us were picked out," said Brian.

"Mr. Taber saw what you did." Tere raised her shoulders. It was so clear to her. "Besides, where you go, trouble follows. You know *dat*!"

"We ought to whip you for having such a smart mouth!" Joe shouted, raising a fist over his head.

"So, what did you tell Mrs. Ferro when you were alone?" Brian spoke more calmly now.

"I told her *dat* I didn't see *anysing* and I don't know too many boys. I'm glad I don't know too many boys." Tere stuck out her chin and knitted her eyebrows.

"Oh, well. Maybe she's telling the truth. Let her by." Brian looked down at the ground and shook his head as though he was giving up. A smile was creeping across his face.

"Let her go over the bridge? No way!" Mary Beth Jackson shouted angrily.

The boys moved back, but Mary Beth Jackson still blocked the way.

"Let her by, Mary Beth," Brian said.

Tere looked just in time to see him wink a message at the others. She knew something was up. They wouldn't let Tere go so easily. Maybe they planned to push her into the ditch when she walked across the footbridge. Tere held tight to her backpack and walked forward.

"Don't let her get away so easily," Mary Beth Jackson shouted at the boys.

Mary Beth Jackson took a few steps backward across the bridge. She faced Tere and took a backward step, with each forward step Tere took. They walked slowly, like tightrope artists performing their act.

Tere had to guard her back. She didn't trust the boys to stand still for long. She turned her head and saw that none had moved. They all watched the action and grinned. But she quickly turned forward again to keep an eye on Mary Beth Jackson.

It was then that Tere noticed something odd about the ground on the other side of the bridge. Where the concrete met the grass, the ground was lower across the width of the path. The grass there had an unnatural quality to it. It seemed to have been placed, rather than grown, in the low area. In places, Tere thought she could see cardboard under the clumps of grass.

It was a trap! The boys had prepared a simple trap for her, as if she were a forest creature without common sense.

Tere and Mary Beth Jackson were almost there. The forward and backward tightrope act continued slowly. Perhaps if Tere had been walking faster and guarding her back she might not have seen the silly trap.

"This is our chance to get even! Don't let her get away!" Mary Beth Jackson shouted to the boys.

Mary Beth Jackson was one backward step away from the trap.

Tere would show them all she couldn't be fooled so easily. She took a quick step toward Mary Beth Jackson, breaking the slow pace. The girl backed up just as quickly. Her foot landed on the hidden cardboard, soggy and curved under the weight of the grass. The soft cover gave way, sending Mary Beth Jackson down into a shallow trench the boys had dug. The sodden cardboard now slipped with her weight, sending her farther down the slimy ditch. Her blond hair picked up dirty grass clumps and her clothes were painted a rich, dripping brown. She rolled to a stop at the muddy bottom, facedown.

"Eeeeeck!" The scream tore through the neighborhood as she lifted her brown, dripping face.

The boys doubled up with laughter. Karl couldn't catch his breath from the spasm of laughter that shook him. Brian pointed a finger down at the figure in the ditch, but no words could come out. Only laughter. Caps were flying. Feet were stomping. They laughed themselves silly.

Mary Beth Jackson looked at them through drippy eyelashes. Even with the mud covering her face, Tere could tell that the knitted eyebrows of anger were about to give way to tears.

Tere felt sorry for her; even if Mary Beth Jackson's last words before the fall had been against her. Maybe it was that Tere understood the feelings of humiliation. Maybe it was that she could have warned the girl but didn't. Tere knew she couldn't just walk away.

Tere jumped across the trap trench to dry ground and set down her backpack. She walked to the edge of the ditch and carefully inched her way down to Mary Beth Jackson.

The muddy figure lying at the bottom looked up, wild-eyed, at Tere.

"Let's get you out of here," said Tere, offering her hand.

Mary Beth Jackson stared at her like a big-eyed chocolate bunny. She kept her mouth shut to prevent mud from running into it.

"Come on. Give me your hand," Tere said steadily. Knowing Mary Beth Jackson, Tere thought, she could easily pull Tere into the muddy bottom. But Tere continued trying to help.

Mary Beth Jackson pushed up against the mess of the ditch bottom. She slowly stood. Mud cascaded down her clothes and dripped into the brown pool making floppy, wet sounds.

The boys watched, entranced. A muffled laugh escaped as they watched the brown goo drip from her clothes.

Tere held out her hand and balanced herself on the bank. Mary Beth Jackson took a tentative step. Her foot made a sucking noise as she lifted it. She looked like a heavy, wading moose. Tere had to fight back a smile.

Finally, Mary Beth Jackson reached for the offered hand. Tere wasn't sure she could pull her out when the slippery, muddy hand slid out of her own. But a second try was successful. Tere grabbed a bush with her free hand and steadied them. The two girls worked their way up the muddy bank slowly. When they reached the top, they were still holding hands.

❧

The girls picked up their packs and walked away together. Neither of them looked back at the boys.

"Thanks," said Mary Beth Jackson. Her shoes squished with each footstep.

Fitting In

Tere shrugged her shoulders. "I couldn't leave you looking like *dat*."

"But I was so mean to you."

"I guess you were."

"I didn't know about the trap. Honest."

"Yeah. If you had known, you would have helped me fall into it."

Thin streams of brown mud ran down Mary Beth Jackson's clothes and skin. Tere tried hard not to laugh at the muddy mess.

"You are leaving a trail of mud." Tere pointed to the sidewalk behind them. "I live a few houses ahead. You can get cleaned up there."

"Thanks. I didn't know you lived so close to me. I live on the next block," Mary Beth Jackson said.

"You do? I don't know if *dat's* good or bad news for me."

Mary Beth Jackson laughed. "I don't blame you for not trusting me. I haven't been very nice to you."

They walked quietly for a while. Only the squishing of the leather shoes and the flopping of the soggy clothes could be heard.

They turned into Tere's yard and walked to the side of the garage, where a hose lay curled on the ground.

"Can I rinse off with this hose?" Mary Beth Jackson asked.

"Wait! Before you do, I will bring you a mirror. You should see what you look like with chocolate hair!" Tere teased.

"Forget it! I just want this goo off me!"

Tere turned on the water and held the hose while Mary Beth Jackson rubbed her face and squeezed her hair. Her T-shirt and shorts dripped brown mud as she scrubbed and wrung the sleeves and any loose fabric she could grip. Slowly, the caked mud gave way to blond wet strands and the light blue of her T-shirt.

"You are looking like a person again," Tere told her. "Take *de* hose while I get a towel for you."

"I hope you're planning to come back this time. Last time you got a towel for me, you ran away!" With hands on her hips, Mary Beth Jackson grinned teasingly.

"Maybe you deserved it. You stole my towel in the locker room." Tere squirted the hose in Mary Beth's face, laughing. "You will just have to trust me."

Mary Beth Jackson took the hose from her. She called out to Tere and squirted the dry girl lightly. "You'll just have to trust me, too."

Tere handed her a towel and the girl wrapped it around her shoulders. They sat on the steps to the kitchen door.

"I didn't mean to leave you *wis* shaving cream over your eyes," Tere said softly. "I got hit on the face, too. I ran to get cleaned up as soon as I could."

"Yeah. I know. I was mad at you for leaving, but I guess I would have done the same thing."

"I don't enjoy being in *de* spotlight and getting messy." Tere shook her head. "But you seem to like it. *De* boys are your friends."

"Not anymore!" Mary Beth Jackson yelled out. "They don't care about anyone but themselves!"

"Well, what *dey* did at *de* carnival was wrong. Now, *dey* want to blame me for *deir* problems."

Mary Beth examined her hands on her lap. "I've been picking on you, too," she admitted quietly.

"It is easy to pick on someone different. My English is not too good."

"Yeah, your words sound different sometimes, but I'm learning you're not so different. You're just like any of us."

Tere picked up Mary Beth's pack. She wiped the mud off it with an old rag.

"I just wish you wouldn't speak Spanish with your friends when others are around," said Mary Beth. "It feels like you're trying to keep something from us."

"Oh, we don't speak Spanish when someone is *wis* us who cannot understand."

"Well, it seems like you're talking about the people around you. It makes me feel uncomfortable."

"We speak Spanish because it's easier for us. Not because we want to talk about *oders*." Tere shook her head.

"Yeah. I suppose the language you learned when you were little would be the easiest to speak."

"I try so hard to say *de* words just right in English. So *de* kids won't laugh at me in class."

"Well, they won't laugh anymore! I'll make sure of that!" Mary Beth looked up at Tere with a serious look on her face.

Tere could tell her new friend meant what she said.

"There's a movie I want to see this weekend. Do you want to go with me?" Mary Beth asked.

"Sure. I love movies." Tere looked up and smiled. Then, she hinted, "I could use your help *wis* my English homework."

"Boy! You sure know how to have fun!" Mary Beth teased.

"Well, I *sought* you could help *wis* the words I cannot say well. I can't even say your name right, Mary *Besf*. See, *dat's* the best I can do!"

"Mary *Beth-th*." She pronounced her own name slowly. "Stick out your tongue and place your upper teeth on it. Now, say 'Beth.'"

Tere followed the directions and attempted it. "Befff. Befff."

"No, no. You've got your teeth on your lips. Try it again. Teeth on tongue."

"*Beth.*" The sound came out softly and slowly. But it was correct.

"You got it!" Mary Beth shouted.

"I feel like I'm spitting when I do *dat*. For Cubans, it's not good manners to make such a sound."

"I guess it is like spitting." Mary Beth laughed. "You'll get used to it and after a while you won't think of it that way."

"Will you teach me to say words *th-the* right way in English?" Tere practiced the new sound.

"Well, correcting people all the time is not good manners for us," Mary Beth let her know.

"You'll be doing it as a way to teach a friend. How can *th-that* be wrong?"

"Sure. I'll be glad to help you," said Mary Beth.

"We can do our homework after *the* movie, if you want."

"Your *th's* sound great!" Mary Beth smiled, happy to have helped. "Maybe we could get together again for school work tomorrow. I could use your help with math."

"It's a deal! We'll have fun first. *Then*, we'll help each *other with-th* school work." Tere smiled proudly.

Tere got her basketball from the garage and dribbled it on the driveway.

"Those boys won't call you *Atena* anymore! I'll make sure of that. Why do you let them?" Mary Beth caught the ball when Tere passed it to her.

"When *th-they* say *things* like that, people show how stupid *they* are. *There's* no need to correct *them. They* can't help being stupid." Tere shrugged. She spoke slowly, to work on the difficult sounds.

"Why do you correct us when we call you Spanish girl, then?" Mary Beth dribbled the basketball. Drops of water splashed off her hair and clothes with every move.

"*That's* not an insult. I'm very proud to be a Cuban girl. You just have to get *the* country right." Tere ran between Mary Beth and the ball and dribbled it away from her friend. Then she threw it back to Mary Beth.

"I'm proud to be an American. I suppose it's like someone calling me 'American girl.'"

"Yeah. But I'm also an American girl. You see, Cuba is part of America. North America. So, when I was born in Cuba, I was also born in America."

"So what does that make me?" Mary Beth bounced the ball in place.

Tere laughed. "I guess you are a United States of America girl!"

❧

Mrs. Baxter had called five students to the board. Each had to solve a problem and give the answer to the class out loud.

Tere trembled as she stood at the front of the class. White chalk dust powdered her right hand. She knew her math problem was right. But she still had to say the answer for all to hear. Tere rehearsed it in her head. Two *thousand*, four hundred and eighty *three*. If she could only get those *th*'s right.

Robbie, a friendly boy, gave his answer. "One hundred fifty five."

"Very good," said Mrs. Baxter.

Now it was Tere's turn. She looked at the class and her eyes spotted Mary Beth. Mary Beth's tongue stuck out of her open mouth, planted on her teeth. She looked funny. Tere tried not to laugh, but a small giggle escaped her.

"Tere, let's see your answer." Mrs. Baxter walked closer to her.

"Two *th*ousand, four hundred and eighty *th*ree." Tere said the numbers carefully. Her teeth had rested on her tongue just right. Her accent was perfect.

"Great," said Mrs. Baxter.

The class was silent. There was no reason to laugh.

Tere winked at Mary Beth. Mary Beth gave her a thumbs-up sign.

❧

Alicia and Mari stared with mouths open at the two girls. Tere and Mary Beth each carried a tray of food and laughed together.

"Can we sit with you?" Tere asked her Cuban friends in English.

Alicia and Mari were too surprised to answer. They just nodded their heads.

"You know my friend Mary Beth, don't you?" Tere asked her friends. "These are my friends, Alicia and Mari."

"Yep! I know you from around school." Mary Beth smiled at the two brown-haired girls.

"I'm glad you remembered the potato chips. Here's your sandwich." Tere handed Mary Beth a plastic lunch bag.

"I love cream cheese and guava jelly, since we ate the mixture at your house this weekend. I asked my mom to buy the stuff for me," Mary Beth said as she chewed a bite from the sandwich Tere had made for her.

Alicia and Mari looked at each other and shook their heads, puzzled at the unlikely friends.

"Mary Beth and I have come up with a great idea."

"Yep," said Mary Beth. She took a quick gulp of her milk. "We're forming a basketball team. Tere and I want you to be on it."

Alicia and Mari looked at Tere with wide-open eyes.

"All of us? On a team?" Alicia asked in disbelief.

"There's Kelly." Mary Beth waved to her. "Come have lunch with us!"

Kelly sat down with the unusual group.

"We're forming a basketball team. Do you want to be on it?" Tere asked the confused girl.

"What do you think we should name it, Tere?" Mary Beth took another bite of her sandwich.

"I've thought of the perfect name." Tere said with a big smile. "The American Girls."

4/97

Connolly Branch Library
433 Centre Street
Jamaica Plain, MA 02130